VIRTUAL
FUTURES

Near-Future Fictions Vol. 1

Edited by
Dan O'Hara, Tom Ward, and Stephen Oram

First published in the United Kingdom, 2018
by Virtual Futures (Est. 1994) C.I.C.
www.virtualfutures.co.uk
@VirtualFutures

Bee Futures by Vaughan Stanger was originally published in
Nature 497, 152 (02 May 2013)

Independent, Superior by Christopher Butera was originally
published on FiresideFiction.com in June 2017

ISBN 978-0-9957882-0-6 (paperback)
ISBN 978-0-9957882-1-3 (ebook)

Editorial Panel: Dan O'Hara, Tom Ward and Stephen Oram
Logo design by: Dan Slavinsky
Cover image by: Celeste Anstruther
Cover design by: Krista Trieu
Formatted by: SilverWood Books

Contact: publishing@virtualfutures.co.uk

Contents

Foreword

On the Origins of Near Future Fictions

A good science fiction story should be able to predict not the automobile but the traffic jam.

Fredrick Pohl

The Virtual Futures Near-Future Fictions series was born after a salon event sometime in February 2017, as fingers wrapped around cool, perspiring glasses and conversational white noise echoed off the neon art in the Lights of Soho gallery in London. Although Virtual Futures has embraced science-fiction since its inception — with Pat Cadigan, Alan Moore, Gwyneth Jones, Hari Kunzru and Geoff Ryman all having graced its stage in its near-twenty-five years of existence — Near-Future Fictions represents the first time that fiction has been the central focus. The series' inspiration came from a desire to provide a creative counterbalance to the theoretical and technical discussions of

Virtual Futures' salon events, a new format that we launched with Semi-Artificial Imagination in 2012. Our first movement toward this creative fusion was inviting Stephen Oram, the current co-director of Near-Future Fictions, to be our Author in Residence for a year; presenting a theme-inspired story before audience questions at expert panels discussing near-future issues such as 'Neurostimulation' or 'Prosthetic Envy'. The synthesis was a success. Stephen's stories grew ever more stimulating. We thought we heard whisperings of something a little larger in audiences' applause.

On that neon evening we decided to let the brainchild crawl out of the womb of a hypothetical event and mature into its own form. At the heart of this new series was a fourfold aim; to reassert the significance of fiction as a valid means of navigating the changes instigated by emerging technologies; to find new sci-fi talent in and outside London, with a stress on diverse authors who were atypical of the scene; to introduce these writers to sci-fi veterans who could help them grow by offering advice and guidance; and to present the result in evenings of short stories speculating on the future in a venue that reflected the unconventionality of the authors.

Three events were planned and executed, each of which demanded authors to submit a 1000-word short story to be read live at the Lights of Soho. The first, 'Interrogating the Future' on March 7 2017, paved the way for later events by opening an alternative discourse to the evangelisation of the future by the tech-elite; it was followed soon after by 'Fit for the Future,' which considered how our fleshy frames may be played with or preyed on in the years to come; and, finally, 'The Laws Don't Apply Here' explored the issues and intricacies that Asimov's famous three commandments raise.

As the audience drifted away from our final event and neon lights turned off one by one, we realised we had completed our goal: the quality of submissions was breathtaking, the incisiveness of the stories haunting. Near Future Fictions had provided a novel space and new place in which new authors could proudly announced their predictions. However, we didn't want to let their visions of the future dissolve into the void of completed live performances with only a Youtube video as a tombstone: we wanted to document our brainchild's first steps, to preserve the stories in print, and to give back to the authors by providing a publication that could help them grow further. In short, we aimed to be a platform in more ways than one.

The following pages display the best stories the three events have to offer. Beginning with the introduction Dr Helen Marshall presented at the series' first event 'Interrogating the Future', in which we are reminded that "we are living in an apocalyptic moment and we have a duty to be witnesses," it proceeds through stories that fall into four broad sections: The Human, The Transhuman, The Posthuman, and the Nonhuman.

While they move further and further away from our human bodies, these stories remain close to home, whispering potent prophesies about what our interaction with technology could do to us in the years to come.

Introduction

On Last Year's Language

Dr Helen Marshall

I wanted to begin with a quotation from T. S. Eliot's poem, 'Little Gidding':

> For last year's words belong to last year's language
> And next year's words await another voice.
> And to make an end is to make a beginning.

The evening's theme is "Interrogating the Future", which seems particularly appropriate for a period of time in which the future seems to be a giant, scary question mark.

I come at this talk from a somewhat strange perspective,

I suppose. I was one of the people – and likely not the only person in this room – who woke up on November 9, 2016 in what seemed to be an alternate reality. I remember logging on that morning and experiencing almost a doubling of vision, as if the universe had split into two tracks that were radically diverging from one another. There was a hallucinatory space of about a week where I still felt as if I could see another world layered underneath mine. I felt shock and disorientation, not a little fear – but also bewilderment at the fragility of the norms and traditions I had come to understand to be bedrocks of reality.

My point in this is not to rehash politics and to vent frustration but to look at this experience critically as a way of thinking about what literature – especially the literature of ideas, the literature of science fiction – *is* and what it ought to do.

A week ago a friend pointed me in the direction of Junot Diaz's excellent article on the earthquake in Haiti which was published in *The Boston Review*. He writes of the etymology of the word *apocalypse*, which means "to uncover and unveil." There are three kinds of apocalypses, he argues: there are those that follow the actual imagined end of the world; there are those that comprise catastrophes which *resemble* the imagined end; and there are those disruptive events that provoke revelation. The apocalypse, he says, quoting James Berger, "is the End, or resembles the end, or explains the end."

We are, by all accounts, no matter where we might fit ourselves in the political spectrum, in an apocalyptic moment. We are witnessing the end of something, or an event that resembles it; we are searching for an account that can explain that end.

On November 9 I had the privilege of teaching a group of MA Short Story writers at my university. It was an evening class. The students had always been a lively bunch, eager, full of questions and comments and jokes and affection for one another. I felt at a loss at how to address them. One colleague had told me not to talk about Trump, to just leave it out of the room, but that seemed impossible. Still, I didn't know what to say.

It struck me as interesting, though, that despite all the anger and anguish I saw on Facebook and Twitter – as if, to quote Obi Wan Kenobi, a million voices were all crying out at once – people were turning to literature for consolation – and for answers. People were discussing *1984* and *Brave New World*; they were quoting from Margaret Atwood's *Handmaid's Tale*; they were welcoming each other to The Hunger Games.

So I told my students the only thing I could reasonably think of to say in the situation, a phrase Ben Markovits, from Royal Holloway, had said: that the purpose of teaching creative writing is, on the one hand, to help students to become published (in the best cases) – but in all cases, regardless of the quality of the writing, it was *to help students to become better witnesses to the world*. And that is what we all are. We are all witnesses to the world. The tools of storytelling can help us, in this respect: they help us to understand our world, to observe it, to *process* it. This is a fundamentally imaginative act and it is an act with great power – the power to witness.

We are living in an apocalyptic moment and we have a duty to be witnesses. We have a duty to observe, to imagine, to speculate, and to create.

Science fiction is a genre that knows about the apocalypse.

I have a new PhD student named Chandra Clarke, and her project argues that although much recent science fiction has been dystopian, we need alternative visions of the future to help us find better ways forward. It is easy to forget that we are also witnessing the beginning of something, a moment whose direction has not yet been fully determined. And the reader of science fiction is, I think, in the best possible position to take advantage of this. That reader's mind has been shaped by the exploration of imaginative worlds, by possible futures, by alternative pasts. The science fiction reader is adept at finding himself – or herself – in a strange new land.

And yet when I find myself speaking to writers of science fiction the one thing I have heard most frequently is how very different the landscape of writing feels at the moment. Our readers don't have the same shared assumptions about reality that we might have counted on a year ago. It seems impossible to write without acknowledging this change.

Gary Dunion on Twitter cleverly captured the zeitgeist by pulling together a number of headlines screengrabbed from the Guardian's feed of "most viewed" articles that day:

- Suspect in North Korea killing "thought she was taking part in TV prank"
- Robert Mugabe could contest election as corpse, wife says
- German parents told to destroy doll that can spy on children

His caption? *Season 4 of Black Mirror is coming along nicely…*
Indeed.

The Twitter account for *Black Mirror* states: "Our job is to explain what's happening to you as best we can." As we have seen in the last eighteen months, it is becoming increasingly difficult to distinguish between fact and fiction. I can only imagine the problem is going to get worse.

And so I go back to T. S. Eliot:

> For last year's words belong to last year's language
> And next year's words await another voice.
> And to make an end is to make a beginning.

This reminds me of an article written by the brilliant but pro-vocative Jonathan McCalmont about the state of weird fiction.

Weird fiction is a strange beast, an eclectic genre, or subgenre. It originated at the turn of the century with the works of authors including Edgar Allan Poe, Arthur Machen, and M. R. James, amongst others and has since developed to include new writers such as China Mieville, M. John Harrison and others. Weird fiction is notable for its generic uncertainty; it is a blend of science fiction and horror (perhaps!) or of literary fiction and horror (perhaps!) or of Lovecraft and whatever happens to be floating close to hand at any given moment (perhaps!).

Michael Kelly of Undertow Press invited me to be the series editor for the fourth volume of *Year's Best Weird Fiction* which reprints material published from the previous year, and so I have needed to grapple with what weird fiction is…

In "Notes on Writing Weird Fiction" Lovecraft stated that his desire in writing weird fiction was to "achieve, momentarily, the illusion of some strange suspension or violation of the galling limitations of time, space, and natural law."

He said:

> These stories frequently emphasise the element of horror because fear is our deepest and strongest emotion, and the one which best lends itself to the creation of nature-defying illusions. Horror and the unknown or the strange

are always closely connected, so that it is hard to create a convincing picture of shattered natural law or cosmic alienage or "outsideness" without laying stress on the emotion of fear. The reason why *time* plays a great part in so many of my tales is that this element looms up in my mind as the most profoundly dramatic and grimly terrible thing in the universe. *Conflict with time* seems to me the most potent and fruitful theme in all human expression.

In this respect, weird fiction seems a perfect vehicle for exploring our present moment. For it does seem to us, I think, to many of us, anyway, that time is out of joint; are we moving back to the happy utopia of the 1950s? Are we moving toward the dystopia of *1984*? Are we returning or progressing? We do not know. We cannot decide. And the possibilities are not so much divergent as layered overtop of one another. We are existing in multiple moments at most, in multiple *times* at once.

And it is *scary*.

Ann and Jeff VanderMeer, in their introduction to *The Weird* compendium recognize the murky taxonomy of weird fiction writing:

Because The Weird often exists in the interstices, because it can occupy different territories simultaneously, an impulse exists among the more rigid taxonomists to find The Weird suspect, to argue it should not, cannot be, separated out from other traditions.

Weird fiction then is used to this strange overlapping, this occupation of simultaneous moments at once. When I asked my students to give me a personal definition of weird fiction there was one – Marian Womack, a wonderful short story writer who had appeared in a previous volume – who had the most interesting answer.

She said:

> We have a long tradition of this in Spain, and this only increased during the dictatorship as new symbolic ways of communicating ideas were rehearsed in narratives (cinematic and literary). This kind of fantasy, in which "something is not quite right", lends itself very well to Gothic sensibility, with its convoluted use of language and its tormented heroes. And then there is an element of irrationality built into the rational and, coming from a Spanish background, I interpret this as surrealism, for me this is a major element I recognize in weird writing, and one that is present in my own understanding of the weird.

This definition struck me as capturing the essence of the weird tale, the embedding of irrationality within the rational: a way of writing which uses the one to expose the other, to make the reader realise that all rational systems are ultimately irrational.

It is a revelatory mode of writing, an apocalyptic mode of writing.

But Jonathan McCalmont! McCalmont traces the history of the resurgence of weird fiction in the twentieth century. In particular, he focuses on several months in 2003 when the TTA Press message boards were alive with a great discussion about the nature of the "New Weird".

The discussion was prompted in part by the success of Mieville who published *The Scar* in 2002 and received critical acclaim in the British Fantasy Award and Locus Awards of 2013. The topic of discussion was the rise of a new type of writing that seemed to have links with the past, but the forum conversations were riven with disputes as to the act of naming. M. John Harrison succinctly summed up the problem:

> If I don't throw my hat in the ring, write a preface, do a guest editorial here, write a review in the *Guardian* there, then I'm leaving it to Michael Moorcock or David Hartwell to describe what I (and the British authors I admire) write.

There was a distinct suspicion of the rise of both the conventional and commercial frameworks which tended to define new "waves" of writing historically and which would go on to attempt to define the nature of the so-called New Weird.

In describing the discussions that took place on that message board, Jonathan McCalmont said something that really struck me:

> Every cultural entity (be it a genre, a sub-genre, a scene, a movement, or a school) is born of a particular place and time…a sudden awareness that the wider culture has changed and that the old tools are no longer up to the job.

I believe we are in one of those moments. The old tools of writing no longer seem up to the job. As T. S. Eliot said, "last year's words belong to last year's language / And next year's words await another voice."

The language I have found for myself is the language of weird fiction, which, in my mind, speaks to the irrationality of our present, floundering systems. We are living in *weird* times; we are seeking to recall a distant, glorified past while we simultaneously rocket toward an uncertain future, with little in the way of maps to guide us.

We need new tools to interrogate the future. We need a new language to understand it, to articulate our concerns, our hopes, our dreams – our possibilities.

The faculty at Anglia Ruskin University put together the Centre for Science Fiction and Fantasy as a way to articulate the value of these genres, which have not always enjoyed the critical and popular appeal they have today.

Science fiction has long provided a way of looking toward the future. It is not intended to predict the future although sometimes it does this. The point of science fiction is to contemplate the future, to renew our hope and our willingness to act—and act wisely. It questions what it means to be human.

I want to end with a story, or a capsule of a story. This comes from the story 'Day of Wrath' published by Sever Gansovsky in 1964 and translated recently by James Womack for *The Big Book of Science Fiction*, edited by the VanderMeers.

Writing at the height of the Cold War, Gansovsky was keenly interested in the absurdities and ruthlessness of human nature. In this story, a biological experiment results in human-like creatures called the Otarks with superior intellectual abilities that terrorize the Russian countryside. A journalist travels to observe the Otarks and quickly finds himself at their mercy. In his final account he begins an article for his newspaper titled: 'What is a Man?'

His optimism, which he had been so proud of, was in the final analysis the optimism of an ostrich. He had just buried his head when it came to the bad news. He read about executions in Paraguay in the newspapers, or about famine in India, but spent his time thinking about how to get money to buy new furniture for his large five-room apartment, or how he might be able to win the good opinion of some important person or other. The Otarks – the Otark-people – shot crowds of protestors, speculated on the price of bread, prepared wars in secret, and he turned away from it all, pretending that nothing of the kind ever happened.

From this point of view, all of his past life suddenly seemed strongly connected with what was now happening to him.

As the journalist approaches his death, he contemplates the final words of his dead companion:

> Maybe it's a good thing that the Otarks have appeared. Now it will become clear what it means to be a man. Now we will all know that to be a man it is not enough to be able to count and to study geometry. There's something else.

The story ends with a chilling conclusion: humanity has defined itself on the basis of its intelligence, and thus established its dominion over other animals. But if a new` race were created, a race of even greater intelligence, how then would humanity define itself? If we were forced to do so, what qualities and attributes would we align ourselves with?

The Otarks are, of course, a metaphor; but they are not only a metaphor. They are a way of posing a question we do face today – just as we faced it in the 1960s: how will science and technology force us to rethink who we are and how we relate to the wider world?

Science fiction is the language of imagining, the language of interrogating. Of asking uncomfortable questions, of challenging dominant ideologies. Of exploring the future, anticipating it, changing it.

We are all witnesses to the world. It is up to us to find our new language, knowing that to make an end is also to make a beginning.

Human

There's Gold in Them Thar Hills, Boys, You Just Need to Know Where to Find It

Nicola Fawcett

It's 2am and I'm 10ft under 5th Avenue, surrounded by some of the most affluent sewage in New York.

Bob, friend and drain engineer, is helping me with my flow cytometer machine, which has spent the last week sorting through the sewage of the rich and famous of condo 1049.

I detach a small flask and stash it carefully in my backpack. There's around 350ml of brownish sludge there, a decent yield. We head back to ground level, where a scrub-down and a change of clothes await, though it'll take about two days to fully remove the smell.

Things I know about Condo 1049 (courtesy of Jules, the

concierge, who likes his whisky on the rocks, and also free):

- Residents include a Ms L. Newington.
- Ms. Newington receives a weekly package from ThermoSci BiomeBestTM.
- The package contains the supplements necessary to maintain a gut full of BiomeBurn microbes, which have an almost unparalleled ability to absorb and metabolise sugars and fats, licensed for the treatment of diabetes.
- This package probably cost Ms. Newington upwards of 7000 dollars.

I also know:

- In the preceding week, Ms. Newington received four deliveries from Carl's Junior, three from Krispy Kreme donuts, eight from Burger King and two from Domino's.
- In this time, she has received 3 visitors, none of whom stayed more than a few hours.
- If Miss Newington is diabetic, she is certainly going about it in a funny way.

The flow cytometer under 5th Avenue has hopefully spent the last week identifying and saving the BiomeBurn microbes which resided, briefly, in Ms. Newington's gut. In an hour or so, I'll have them in a container of dry ice, on their way to the ChemQuik lab in Mexico, and I'll be a thousand dollars or so the richer. It's not exactly how I imagined myself using my PhD in molecular biology, but it certainly pays the bills in a way a PostDoc position at Columbia spectacularly doesn't. You may ask why these microbes are quite so valuable. Let me recount a bit of history.

ThermoSci first managed to engineer super sugar-and-fat-burning microbes over 10 years ago. They turn out to be great at curing mice with diabetes, and easy to control with antibiotics. Unfortunately, nature being what it is, it didn't take long for these microbes to start sharing genes with other gut microbes, learning to evade control and generally misbehave. I guess the experience with Monsanto's GM crops should have made this a rather obvious development. So someone at ThermoSci had a brainwave – don't use regular microbes, use xenomicrobes. These synthetic microbes were made out of molecules not found in nature – xenonucleic acids and xenopeptides. Being so completely different, they couldn't talk or share or recombine with anything else, and they required regular supplementation of these xeno-nutrients to survive. Stop the supplements, the xeno-microbes die, and normal microbes return. Job done.

Headlines of 'Synthetic Microbes Cure Diabetes' (in mice) were shortly followed by convenient media stories like 'My father died of diabetes, why is the FDA blocking this miracle treatment?' The fast-tracked human trials happily confirmed these xeno-microbes, (now branded as ThermoSci BiomeBurn), could cure humans of diabetes, with the interesting side effect of significant weight loss, despite the trial participants eating pretty much whatever they wanted.

Of course, treatment didn't come cheap. Xenobiotic manufacture is a complicated process. The economic burden of diabetes was over $250 billion in the US. Diabetes meant a lifetime of blood tests, injections, complications. Compared to that, what was fifty, maybe a hundred thousand dollars?

The sudden epidemic of previously-undiagnosed diabetes among the portion of the population with fifty thousand to spare was second only to the sudden epidemic of private diabetologists interested in diagnosing diabetes, pre-diabetes, almost-diabetes, and even could-one-day-turn-into-diabetes.

If, however, you had diabetes but not the spare fifty thousand, like, say, 400 million people or 8% of the world, you might think for a second that it would be really great if maybe others could develop and improve things, maybe make alternative treatments. Except for the fact that ThermoSci published the bare minimum, and patented the hell out of it all. Legal fucking fortress. You work for ThermoSci or you go home. Heck, you couldn't even grow the bugs to study them.

That said, if you could get your hands on the bugs, you could purify them into the xeno-nutrients required. You just need to find a source, such as a convenient BiomeBurn patient. After all, bugs go in one end, bugs come out the other end.

ThermoSci tried to claim ownership of the 'end product' so to speak, but the Supreme Court reaffirmed that a patient is legally the owner of their own human tissue, and as such, their own shit, and could do what the hell they like with it. ThermoSci responded by putting their prices up, and offering huge rebates for patients who returned their carefully collected 'end products'.

However, happily for me (as it turns out), a certain section of society for whom money is no object preferred instead to continue to crap how, where, and when, they wished. Equally happily, once into the public sewer system, the material ceases to be their, or ThermoSci's, property.

If you're not ThermoSci, and you want to study the bugs, or maybe you want to treat your diabetes at a fraction of the cost, or maybe you want to treat your weight too, then ChemQuik Mexico is who you contact. ChemQuik pay handsomely to those who can find supplies of BiomeBurn microbes. If they're less-than-forthcoming on their advertising about their sources, one can understand it.

So, if you take a 'repurposed' flow cytometer your lab is throwing out, a battery pack, add thirty dollars in drinks for a Manhattan concierge on the lookout for BiomeBurn parcels, in no time at all, you've got yourself a tidy earner.

Yesterday Jules mentioned he'd seen a number of ChemQuik packages going to the condo next door. I might have to set up another collection point. After all, what God giveth, God taketh away, and possibly giveth back again, in easy-to-swallow capsule form.

Bee Futures

Vaughan Stanger

Having counted his thirtieth bumblebee corpse of the morning, Farmer Giles could no longer deny that the Battle of Sheldon Farm had begun.

He trod the scorched remains into the turf while gazing at the nearest apple tree. By rights, its blossom-laden branches ought to be thick with bees. Sadly, today's inspection of the orchard had revealed none; at least none still alive. At this rate there would be hardly any Braeburns for his pickers to harvest come September. And the same would hold true for his pears, raspberries, tomatoes and courgettes.

Until now Farmer Giles had given little credence to the

local rumour mill's mutterings about laser-equipped robo-wasps. But faced with the destruction of his genetically optimised pollinators, he could no longer deny the reality of the situation. Now that GM wheat production had ceased throughout the UK, the bio-Luddites were turning their firepower on the Weald of Kent's fruit and vegetable growers.

Why do we bother?

His inadvertent broadcast over AgriNet brought an instant reply, buzzing deep inside his head.

Because farming's what we do, brother!

As usual, Farmer Jones spoke the truth.

Amen to that!

If the people of this increasingly brown and unpleasant land were to enjoy their usual cornucopia of foodstuffs, farmers like him would have to find a way to win the war.

After finishing his day's labour, Farmer Giles liked to relax by watching wartime documentaries beamed directly into his head by the History Channel. From these he understood that determined attack usually overcame stubborn defence.

Still, he had quotas to fulfil, with heavy penalties from Asda if he failed to deliver. So he ordered a new batch of pollinators — this time an artificial variety equipped with laser stings.

The bee did not stir when Farmer Giles brushed his toes against it. On this occasion he could discern no signs of scorching. Given the absence of a diagnostic data feed, he concluded that an EM pulse had fried the robot's tiny brain.

Alerted by a motion detector flashing red in his peripheral vision, Farmer Giles strode out of the orchard. As he approached

Sheldon Farm's eastern boundary, he discarded his stealth cloak. A gangly, shaven-headed man and a stouter, dark-haired woman, both dressed in camouflage gear, looked up from their mil-spec tablets.

"You'll never stop me farming" he told them.

It was what he did. He knew no other purpose.

The pair gawped at him. Perhaps it was his nakedness that startled them. But why wear clothes when one was sustained by sunlight?

And why grow food for people who didn't deserve it?

The man shrugged. "Your wheat-growing friends in Norfolk said the same thing."

"I can always buy more pollinators."

Now the woman chipped in. "And we'll destroy them, too. We won't give up until you *stop* planting GM crops. You'll run out of money long before we do!"

Which was doubtless true, Farmer Giles mused. Plus the local police had long since given up any pretence of defending his land. Was this a war really worth fighting? Faced with a financially ruinous escalation in insectile hostilities, he nodded his acquiescence.

"Okay then; I'll think about it."

"Well, all right!" The woman looked startled at the ease of her victory.

Farmer Giles turned away from his persecutors.

He would just have to find another way to turn a profit.

The truth was unpalatable, but could not be denied.

Growing non-GM fruit and vegetables made no financial sense. Non-GM plants cost too much; the required fertiliser levels were illegal; the yields too low.

Farmer Giles gazed at the meadow daisies, flourishing despite the heat.

I think I'll try flowers.

With continental growers struggling to maintain supplies due to summer droughts, he felt confident he'd identified a profitable new niche.

Farmer Jones snorted his contempt. *Well, I'm switching to biofuel maize. There's profit in that, for sure. Good luck with your blooms, though.*

Good luck to you, too!

Farmer Giles suspected his neighbour would need something a lot stronger than luck to repel the swarms of pests migrating from the Mediterranean, but he decided to keep his counsel.

In any case, he had seeds to order.

After depositing two baskets of freshly-cut flowers on a fold-up table, Farmer Giles leaned against Sheldon Farm's main gate and waited for the next group of refugees to arrive. His bee count had reached ten before a 4x4 parked up.

Biofuel supplies remained plentiful, evidently.

Two people got out of the vehicle. A gaunt-faced, dark-haired woman clutched the hand of a whimpering child. Farmer Giles realised he'd seen her before. He guessed that the anti-GM campaigner's partner had deserted her shortly after the supermarkets closed their doors for good.

The woman stared at the flowers before turning despairing eyes on Farmer Giles.

"Haven't you got any food?"

Farmer Giles shook his head while sliding a tulip stem above the boy's left ear.

The woman frowned. "What's *that* for?"

"Something for the journey," he said.

The boy had started munching on the offering even before his mother could drag him away from the baskets. Farmer Giles gave a sorrowful shake of his head. He had hoped people would choose to die wearing flowers in their hair, but that rarely happened.

These days he didn't have the heart to ask for money.

Inside, Outside

Allen Ashley

Jayden had undergone two penis enlargements followed by one reduction. The operations had been undertaken by two robo-docs who had turned up at his pod complete with tools, anaesthetics, dressings and super-silicone. Of course, he had wanted to be as impressive as everybody else on the Skippy-sex sites but recent research and, indeed, personal experience had shown that having too much length and girth interfered with the daily fitness requirements.

He enjoyed his bouts of Skippy-sex. Technically, they were masturbation sessions with a video-link to a distant partner, usually at least partially unclothed in order to show off their robo-sculpted bikini bodies. As well as their de rigueur pendulous breasts and lightened hair, his favourites amongst these available women might also sport a feminine tattoo: a butterfly on the left shoulder, a mermaid or two on the inner thigh. So long as you sat perfectly still, the laser from the home screen could execute most designs perfectly. Sometimes Jayden wondered what it would be like to actually couple with a willing partner *in the flesh*. The government's Anti-Contact Legislation twelve years ago had forbidden physical intimacy at all levels of society. Even mothers and babies didn't snuggle together anymore. It was healthier for the child to be monitored and raised by artificially intelligent, and clearly superior, nurses and teachers.

Jayden's memories – of attending school and shaking hands with, bumping into or hanging around with so-called friends – were a bit hazy these days. Like it was another life; now gone. The films he watched while he trained on his fit-monitor still showed people in close proximity but were composed of manipulated images. Sports events were one-on-one affairs; tennis matches, mostly. Team sports had died with the advent of the no touching rules. You wanted to stay alive and avoid ill-health, didn't you? It was bad enough having to carry around your own bacteria without being infected by somebody else's.

He was wearing comfortable, loose sports clothing. The pod's heating was set at its regular level and he could have trained without any clothes had he wished but wearing the right gear kept him in the zone. He set the treadmill to time him on his regular morning 5K run.

A noise outside distracted him. It was almost certainly the delivery drone pushing into his pod airlock with a fresh batch of supplies. But it put him off his stride and now, even if he pounded against the plastic pads, he was never going to achieve a new personal best. Never mind, just focus on the screen projection of passing conifer trees and let the tempo of his chosen music keep him on track.

Abruptly, everything faded, ceased. He gripped the side bars to stop himself falling over from residual momentum. It was dark in the pod, uncomfortably so; an emergency red light flashed on and an automated voice advised him to exit the property immediately.

"Follow protocol," it shrieked to the arriving backbeat of a two-note alarm.

The system must be battery-operated or some such retro shit, he decided. He crossed to his door and tried the internal manual lever. It was stiff from disuse, or he was out of the habit, but it opened on the fourth wrench.

He was alone in the corridor. The logo of a green walking figure alerted him to the location of the exit. He headed that way. He had been cooped up indoors so long that he hadn't remembered that he lived on the third floor. Common sense told him to head down. Even so, he found the descent more challenging than he'd anticipated and almost lost his footing on three occasions. His flat level workouts hadn't prepared him for this eventuality.

A push on the door and he was outside in an uncomfortably agoraphobia-inducing space. The floor was grey, hard, dirty but clearly not natural. His googly lenses were having trouble adjusting to the changed light. And there were *other people* around, too, which simply added to Jayden's confusion. The men looked mostly similar to his own stored image – toned, muscled, wearing a singlet, sneakers and shorts. The women uniformly sported dyed blonde hair, their micro-waists and stick-like sculpted legs doing their best to keep their top-heavy bodies upright. A few were attempting to cover their bikinis with shreds of fabric to preserve a modesty important in the personal world that was largely absent in the virtual.

Jayden blinked three times, hoping his lenses would reset. To his left he spied some large metal objects, their paint flaking. Although they were nothing like the visuals on the latest games, he realised these must be vehicles. Which meant he was standing in that most retro of locations: a car park.

Before he could ponder further, the silent spell was broken by a man over to his right.

"Shit, is that actual sunshine up there? It's going to give me cancer. Or ruin my tan."

A woman to Jayden's immediate left, with a towel wrapped around her shoulders, responded, "Hey, guys, we're out in the open air. It'll be toxic. I don't think I can breathe."

As if to confirm her fears, she began coughing. Jayden was worried that he might have to support her in some way, which would breach the anti-touching laws. A fit wracked her body, revealing a butterfly tattoo on her shoulder. Jayden recognised her as an ex-Skippy-sex partner. In real life, her complexion was patchy and her super-enhanced breasts looked likely to overbalance her at any moment.

The tension was broken by a repeated, robotic announcement: "All clear. Return to dwellings immediately."

At first there was a rush and an almost collision. Then everybody remembered the legislation and allowed large gaps to form in the still-hurrying queue.

"After you, neighbour," Jayden said to the coughing woman.

"Why, thank you, Jay24XB." The tightened skin of her fingers reached towards him…until she thought better of it. "Skip with me later, boy," she added, heading breathlessly for the first floor.

36

Young Blood

Jule Owen

Cam's younger brother, Val, was unconscious on the floor between the sofa and the coffee table. He was surrounded by the others, Caine who was there for the home-brew, and Jane, who Caine had gone to fetch when he found out what was happening because he thought she knew CPR.

"It was a long time ago," she said forlornly, crouching over Val's inert body, trying again to breathe into his mouth and press his chest. "I only did it to a doll."

Cam was hanging on the line to the hospital. He managed to get 30 free seconds with a bot at the call centre, but it wasn't enough time to explain what had happened and tell them where to send the ambulance. They knew the address already, of course. They also knew 30 seconds is too short a time to gather details in an emergency, but frustrating people is how they got customers to upgrade. Because Cam had used the word 'emergency', in addition to the usual commercial, he had to listen to a message up-selling from the ad-funded version of LifeGuard, Cam's healthcare service, to the first paid tier, which only had ads in non-emergency calls. Cam couldn't even afford that.

"His brain is probably dead by now," Caine said, looking down sceptically at Val. "His heart stopped beating ten minutes ago."

"How do you know when his heart stopped beating?" Jane said, scornfully.

"He's blue!" Caine said.

"I heard there was a man who was kept alive for over an hour through CPR," Jane said, giving his chest another push. She was getting tired.

"Bullshit. Val's dead. Cam may as well end that call and get on to the undertaker."

"We need to send him to the hospital anyway, even if he's dead," Jane said.

Caine pulled a sceptical face. "What's the point? It'll only cost Cam money."

"Why are you such an insensitive shit? He's Cam's brother, for god's sake!" Jane was getting angry.

Caine explained, "Cam never really liked him. And Cam's my friend and he's alive. I don't want him bankrupted."

Jane sighed, trying to be patient. She said, "Cam will need to get a death certificate from a doctor."

"Can't we just get Dr Kim?" Caine asked. "He's a few

blocks down and he'll do it for a fraction of the price."

"He's not a real doctor," Jane said. "Struck off. Why else would he be working here?"

"Will you shut up!" Cam said, turning from the speaker. "He's not dead!"

"I'm sorry, will you repeat that?" the bot asked as the commercial cut off suddenly. "Did you say 'he's not dead'?"

"No he's not dead," Cam repeated. "We need an ambulance, quickly. Heart attack."

"Address please."

Cam gave his address and another ad started. "Amaranth Corporation would like to invite you to live forever," it said.

"Jeeze," Caine said. "Have those arseholes in the Amaranth marketing department even been to Basic? Why the hell would anyone stuck here in this hell hole want to live forever? What kind of crap targeting do they have on their advertising?"

"It's all rubbish anyway," Jane said. "They just con people with more money than sense into having their blood replaced with the blood of young people."

"No way!" said Caine.

"It's true! Some crazy scientist says it rejuvenates your cells and makes you live longer. They injected mice with the plasma portion of blood from young mice. It made the old mice able to learn again. Now they do it to people."

"Where do they get the blood?"

"Shut up, will you?" Cam shouted. "I need to concentrate in case the bot comes back on the line."

"Imagine if you had all the time in the world," the ad was still saying, beaming its silken voice through the speakers in the apartment. These were the ones fitted by the landlord that you couldn't remove without getting evicted. The landlord got money from the ad companies, of course. That is how the rent was kept so low, so they all said.

The ad continued, "A lifetime to play, another lifetime to study, the one after that for adventure and travel."

"Please give your address." The LifeGuard bot's robotic voice cut rudely into the fantasy the ad had created.

"I just did!" Cam said, knowing he shouldn't lose his temper, but becoming increasingly frustrated and desperate.

"We have no record of that."

Cam garbled the address again quickly, managing to get it in before the end of the 30 seconds and receiving a metallic "Confirmed," before another ad began.

"In need of credit?" the ad said. "Amaranth needs blood. If you are under twenty-five and healthy, this might be your lucky day! We offer incredible rewards for lifetime contributors."

"I can't believe they…" Caine started.

"For Peter's sake shut up will you!" Cam bellowed.

"I'm so sorry, Sir," the nurse said, switching off the TV in Cam's hospital room. "I'm not sure what happened. I'll get a technician to deal with it immediately. You really shouldn't be seeing ads. Can I get you something to read in the meantime?"

Cam shook his head and looked out of the room onto the parkland view. There were more trees than he'd ever seen in his life.

"I'm sorry about your brother," she said.

Cam shrugged. "He was braindead on arrival. Nothing anyone could do."

"Still, it must be good to know he's making a positive contribution to other people's lives now."

Cam thought of his brother's body hooked up to the

life-support machine downstairs. After Cam had signed the consent forms, he'd watched as Val had been connected to the Amaranth Corporation Blood Farm machine. It was now taking Val's blood as fast as he could make it. Cam glanced at the machine next to him, pumping that young blood into him.

The nurse said, "He had such an unusual blood group. So lucky you were a match!"

"Yeah, wasn't it?" Cam said.

Transhuman

Cries and Bionic Eyes

A. Umbra

Part 1

In a 7th floor apartment in East London, on a bloodstained, floral sofa, a topless boy with a tattoo of a dog's paw on his ribs lay suspended in a private ecstasy of tears. He had spent the day binging on the teary sadness often promoted by opening a cheap bottle of red wine before 12 o'clock, watching shakily filmed memories of a first lover's felicities projected on a grimy wall, and writhing while his shoulders were attached to the bare curtain-rail above him by fishhooks and wires — making his back look like it had angel's wings that had been amputated.

An orange butterfly sucked on his brown iris through the small gap between his almost closed eyelids. He opened them wider when he saw its wings flap through the slit, took a photo with the camera built into his eye, and — having crushed it between his fingers and thrown the twitching frame across the room — returned to the euphoria of his post-fix cocoon.

The boy hadn't always been like this. The sofa used to be stained with the smells of a busy, happy house; the spaghetti bolognese his mum cooked when she visited, his girlfriend's sweet perfume, sweaty friends…

Before the Wide Eyed eyeball had been installed on his 22nd Birthday, which had lead to this teary stagnation, no one had seen him cry since he was 13. He had resented the thought of how weak his broad frame would have looked being wracked and spasmed by sobs. Now, he didn't care. As he flexed his shoulders, pulling the skin another few centimetres away from the musculature, he felt a tear roll down his cheek as he thought back to the day that he had resolved to never cry again…

Morning service in the school's modernist chapel. 653 boys sung out of tune. As the closing notes of 'All Things Bright and Beautiful' died in the rafters, his text alert signal had bounced off the walls. Followed by his ugly inhalation and cracked cry. His Mum had sent him five words.

"Luke's dead. I'm sorry, love."

His Labrador was gone. The only living thing that knew all his problems; because animals can never say the wrong thing back. By lunchtime boys in the year above him were selling little bottles labelled 'Genuine Crybaby Tears' for 20p outside the dining room. "Roll up and grab your tears ladies and gentlemen — they bring pets back from the grave".

The projector clicked and faded to black, interrupting his

recollection — the memories of his ex had run out. So had the red wine. She was one among a crowd of people who had tried to rescue him from the apathetic fog of his chronic crying since that fateful 22nd Birthday — his mother had coughed pleadings about childhood innocence, his friends had blackmailed him emotionally — but it was her words, "you used to be so beautiful," that stuck in his head like the hooks in his shoulders, that made him saddest.

So, the videos of her were the ones he used to make himself cry most frequently.

He grabbed the remote controller, navigated to Netflix, and within seconds had found the 'Favourites' section. The title sequence of *The Notebook* started to play as he pulled a long piece of barbed wire out of a salad bowl full of disinfectant and began to wrap it around his arm.

Part 2

'Wide-eyed', the company that had first cracked the enigma of how to integrate video and photo hardware into a bionic eyeball that wouldn't be rejected by the body, had been understandably idiotic in three interconnected respects when developing eyes fit for the future of social media:

> Firstly, due to tight budgets, an increasingly overshot deadline, and the practical necessities of perfecting the mechanisms of the basal and reflexive tears, they had forgotten to incorporate the emotional tear into their design. Their final product could lubricate the eyeball, and clean it when necessary, but it could not provide the therapeutic effect of the emotional

tear. When one of the employees reached the tragic conclusion of *Titanic* without crying for the first time in his life, leaving him in an emotional limbo, the company realised too late that their design lacked the necessary integration to carry cortisol, prolactin and other stress inducing hormones out of the brain — the role that the emotional tear serves.

Secondly, because they didn't realise this until the product was being implemented, they tried a quick-fix to prevent a PR shitstorm. Some bright spark in the boardroom suggested the idea of giving an active kick, "a high", out of crying by providing some kind of counter-pleasure when a tear was shed in order to simulate the relief of emotional tears. It was the best idea they had — and they had to act fast. The eyes were reprogrammed remotely, and a newly synthesised opiate — which had proven to match the calming effects of crying in lab conditions — was added to the bottles customers had to fill their bionic eyes with on a daily basis. The idea was simple: when sufficient stress hormones were detected, the eye released a small quantity of the drug. Problems would only arise if the people with Wide Eyes were imprudent enough to use the mechanism recreationally – which could lead to an addictive relationship with pain.

Thirdly, they hadn't considered the response of the Julia Butterfly, one of the few insects known to get its necessary sodium from the secretions of other animals – tears, piss, sweat. When two of the butterflies escaped on a Hello Kitty backpack from The Natural History Museum's Sensational Butterflies exhibition, it didn't take the species long to propagate by feeding off the tears of addiction or the sweats of withdrawal prominent in our city due to the epidemic of crying-addiction; although the opiate in the perspiration killed the insects in a few days. While more of society grew more creative in their methods of masochism — for tears of pain are easier to summon than tears of joy — corpses of butterflies began to stack up on the streets, where they were crushed by the soles or heels of business shoes in the morning, the paws of dogs in the afternoon, or cruel schoolboys' trainers in the evening.

Truth and What Comes After

L. P. Lee

All day long my bullshit detector was going off. I was a trial user for TrustMe, a new start-up specialising in devices that monitored the nuances of a person's speech. You'd plug it into your ear like a hipster hearing aid, and it would give you a little beep whenever it picked up a suspicious change in your interlocutor's 'base line'.

The problem was that an office is not a hospitable place to trial a bullshit detector.

By the end of the day my ears were ringing and I shuffled in exhaustion towards the lift and freedom.

I got in the lift and in came Kyle. Please don't open your

mouth, I thought. Just don't. Then I realised that he was also sporting one of the devices.

"These are terrible, aren't they?" He said. He looked a little grey in the face.

"What happened to you?" I asked.

"Sex with my girlfriend," he said.

Back home I realised that I didn't really need a device when good old gut feelings did me just fine. It was certainly interesting though to have the hunches one so often ignored confirmed by a hearing aid.

I unhooked the device and placed it on the table. It sat there like a coiled snake.

It'll never take off, I thought.

It went viral right after launch. Everyone had to have one. Not that you could tell: the latest model was so discreet that you wouldn't always know if someone was wearing it.

From anxious parents checking out their babysitter's background to cautious, probing mother-in-laws, little beeps were going off in a multitude of ears every day.

There was speculation that sooner or later the devices would be allowed in a court of law, and that police investigations were already beginning to make use of them.

A new style of political communication emerged: monosyllabic answers were in vogue and, for the first time, flat silences and clipped answers were becoming a real issue in live broadcasts. The era of grandiose posturing and flippant chatter seemed to be over.

Worried that I would be at a disadvantage without one, I ended up buying into it again, but it was like being sucked into a whirlpool of escalating social anxiety. The truth simply didn't cut it in each and every situation. Left and right couples were breaking up, old people were shaking walking sticks at each other, and redundancies were mushrooming.

Meanwhile, there was a political movement growing whose leader set off all of our bullshit detectors. Young and full of irrepressible energy, Rufus Quibblestone bounced from scandal to scandal, his followers multiplying on all of the social media channels.

It must have given people a headache, watching him on the telly with their detector beeping in their ear all the time. I had to just take it out whenever he appeared on the news. Come to think of it, I couldn't imagine what it would be like at his rallies: just waves of irritated people clenching their eyes shut, dealing with their self-inflicted migraines. How did they do it, and how could he persist when we all knew he was lying?

Soon enough came the answer, and my biggest shock so far. The cameras caught Quibblestone in a blistering rant against the status quo, the elites who were engaged even in the falsifying of truth. Real truth. The sun lit and haloed his platinum hair, his blue eyes blazed in his child-like face.

He waved a bullshit detector in the air, and he said, "This is the epitome of false truth propagated by the invested elite," and he threw it down from the stage, and it bounced on the ground and broke, and the platter-eyed crowd erupted into wild applause and jubilant cheering. And they threw down their own devices, and trampled them into the dirt.

Spring arrived and I began suffering from moments of acute disorientation. Sometimes it was as if I was witnessing the world shattering and being pieced together again in wilfully incorrect arrangements that distorted what was once so familiar, rendering it no longer recognisable.

From my smaller and colder apartment, I docked more points off my citizen score by logging onto a liberal news site and watching the latest interview with the CEO of TrustMe. A young ex-Physicist, ex-Google wunderkind, Dr Julia Kowalski had a polite and calm exterior and a gentle way of talking. Only her earnest, glittering eyes revealed a soul aflame.

TrustMe was swamped in scandal again: while the company insisted that their bullshit detector had undergone rigorous testing and was 99.9% accurate, Quibblestone was taking time out from his new PM duties to publicly decry Dr Kowalski a phoney.

Certainly consumers had turned against bullshit detectors, because these days they were always going off, all the time. There was no rest from the device's endless nudging.

Responding to the interviewer's questions, Dr Kowalski said, "the issue is not the quality of our product, it's that consumers' demands are changing."

Afterward I went out to pick up milk, and bumped into my old colleague Kyle on Upper Street. We both drew breath in surprise at each other's changed appearance. His cheeks were bursting with dewy vitality, his mouth curved upwards in a perpetual smile. He wasn't walking along Upper Street, he was practically skipping.

"Christ," he said, casting a concerned eye over my deflated form. "You could do with a bit of HappyAid."

"What the hell is that?"

He tapped his ear and said, "It filters what you hear based on your worldview. It basically helps you take back control."

"That sounds shit," I said.

"Yeah it's great, isn't it?" He said.

He clapped my shoulder. "Well, cheerio!" He said, and skipped off.

As soon as I got home, I signed up for HappyAid.

Gourmet Hunger

Jackie Kingon

Come to New Chicago, Mars' capital, and eat at my restaurant, Molly's Bistro. Mars Media gave it: four spiral galaxies.

But not today. My husband Cortland and I are invited to Virtual Vitals — a virtual restaurant where holographic smoke and mirrors recreate the experience of fine restaurant dining — for a virtual meal before their opening.

"Welcome to Virtual Vitals," a tall man says. "I'm Avery, head waiter. Please follow me."

We walk through a quiet white room. Cortland says, "This place looks like it was plastered in the stuff used for death masks."

Avery says, "We want no distractions."

"Better to fry our brains," Cortland says.

The room is divided into cubicles. Each has people seated around tables covered with white linen cloths, white china, and crystal glasses. Most are poking at floating coloured menus. Avery stops at an empty cubicle and gestures for us to step inside. We sit. A moment later, floating screens appear at eye level.

"We have over fifty thousand choices on the menu," Avery says. "If you don't find what you want, we can create it."

I ask, "Any recommendations or specials?"

"Everything is special. Touch the screen, make your selections. Someone will come and assist you. Enjoy your meal." Avery leaves.

Cortland says, "Why do I feel like we're in a horror movie?"

"Because maybe we are," I whisper.

A waiter pours water into our glasses.

"Is this water real?" I ask.

"Yes. We thought real water added a nice touch."

I sip the water.

"How does it taste?" Cortland asks.

"Like water."

"Anything special about it?"

"Not that I can tell."

He pushes his glass away.

A few moments later, owner Rick Frances, and a woman in a lab coat holding a white case approach.

"Molly! Cortland!" Rick says, arms outstretched as though we're old friends. "Meet Lena Fermi, my chief engineer and brains behind Virtual Vitals. She makes everything run the way it should."

We smile.

"What did you think of the menu?" Rick asks.

"Overwhelming," I say. "I thought I knew food, but you have food I've never heard of."

Lena says, "We can combine taste combinations and foods even if they physically don't exist."

Rick turns to Cortland. "Aren't you the president of Molawn Music – and aren't The Lunar Tunes your daughters?"

Cortland nods.

"And it's an honor to have *the* Molly of Molly's Bistro."

I smile.

Rick says, "Let me explain how Virtual Vitals works. Everything is electronically coded. We scanned you when you sat in these chairs."

Cortland jumps up. "You scanned us?"

"Relax. Settings are deleted when you get up so we can use the chair again."

Cortland sits.

Rick says, "Items on the table are keyed to the virtual experience through haptic holograms. The tactile illusion is generated by the pressure of sound waves. Everything is connected to our main computer. When the program is engaged, you'll feel sensations that mimic the push and pull of a knife and fork cutting food. When you lift your fork or spoon and put it in your mouth, you'll have the sensations that mimic the real thing. In fact, Molly, you can eat your restaurant's food. We programmed your menu and that of other restaurants. Want a Jovian burger? Saturnian slider? No problem. But we're not stealing recipes; we're electronically reinterpreting food."

Cortland lifts a tablespoon and examines it. "So this thing is rigged? Feels like a regular spoon."

"It was once," Lena says. Then she opens her case, removes

a headset and gloves, and demonstrates how the equipment is used.

Cortland says it reminds him of a flight attendant giving instructions for an emergency.

She holds a headset in front of me.

"Does it hurt?" I ask.

"Of course not," she says. "Now how does it feel?"

"Hardly know I'm wearing it."

She does the same for Cortland, who looks like he's tolerating a medical exam.

Lena says, "You'll be so engrossed you won't be aware of anything artificial. Signals are sent to your taste buds so the perception of 'eating' will be coordinated with what you do with your eyes, hands, and mouth."

"What if we don't like what we're eating?" Cortland asks.

"Say 'new menu' and a new menu will appear in front of you."

Cortland nods. "What happens when I say the word 'help'?"

"Say 'stop' and the program will disengage."

When the 'meal' ends, Cortland drains his water, and says, "was that as good as I thought it was, Molly?"

"Better."

Cortland says, "If that were a real experience and not a virtual one, Virtual Vitals would put every restaurant I know out of business. Did you have the butter cookie cone filled with white chocolate gelato with thick hot chocolate sauce in the bottom bit?"

"Three," I say. "Rick deserves lots of credit. Diabetics can eat sweets, food allergists gorge on forbidden foods and alcoholics drink alcohol with impunity. But I'm starving! Starving!"

When we get home we rush to the kitchen. We eat everything. Everything! Tomato paste straight from the can, frozen vegetables from the freezer, vanilla extract and Worcestershire sauce. Don't say *ugh* until you know what starving feels like.

The following week, Virtual Vitals officially opens. When the first 'meal' ends and people are as hungry as we had been, they run into Molly's Bistro like they heard the words 'free beer'.

So regarding my headwaiter's question: 'Will a virtual restaurant be good or bad for good food?', I'll let you be the judge.

The Department of Re-pairing

Jane Norris

The Doctor looked out of the window of her new office, and thought of her previous field work – repairing transmitters in outlying areas where it was difficult to get a signal. She had been surprised by her move through the departments, from a peripheral 'Identifier', to middle ranking 'Analyst', to inner 'Translator', before having finally achieved a coveted central position of 'Senior Connector'. But then she had worked hard at amplifying her skills, tuning her ability to pick up a wide band of resonance, enhancing her sensitivity to the faintest vibration. Her nickname in the field had been 'the Queen of Wi-Fi'. These days of course one didn't build one's career in a narrow progressive way: gone were the chains of qualifications, the graduation from a lower level to a higher one that was deemed 'more advanced' leading to a focused specialism, until sitting at the top of a leafless tree of knowledge was a lone research professor writing in isolation, their dislocation from society ensured by an elite faculty. No, that was too linear and old school.

She thought back over the last ten years. There had been considerable confusion and disorientation – the shift from hierarchy to aerial view, from 'pyramids to pancakes'…one of the many phrases that sought to clarify the difficult gear change everyone had been through. Perhaps more a slipping of gears altogether, she thought. The final collapse of Enlightenment conceptual structures had happened in the shadows of the manufacturing disintegration during the mid 2020s. The irony had escaped no one that that was *the era* that should have had perfect vision (if you measured everything numerically of course).

She liked to refer to her ability in this new age of 'pairing' as a continuation of the old skill of matrimonial matchmaking, only now it was between human/trans-human/bio-object and the few remaining object-objects. There was precious little pure bio left. She glanced out of the side window towards her old lab and considered yet again how far pairing had come.

Sensing Mary come into the room, she turned to smile. They had had a difficult day yesterday, the incident at the Milan Design Fair had been troubling and had caused some tensions between them. It was important to regroup.

"These are broken, old Thonet chairs, they're rubbish!" Mary said.

The Dr jumped and mentally fast-forwarded through the usual pleasantries…

"Surely we don't have to repair *everything*…" Mary continued.

"But our Department…" the Dr started…

"…in the Whole World!" Mary finished rolling her eyes.

The Dr closed hers, and tried to consider the Intern's outburst, searching for a comment that was not going to make the situation worse…(Somewhere in Nairobi a request for chairs pinged up on a screen – she tried to ignore it). This was not about actual chairs, and they were not what needed re-pairing at this moment. She gathered her thoughts carefully.

"Is it the style – the dark bent wood…?"

"No! I am just tired of trying to rescue every bit of rubbish from the Selfi age, pretending it has a use – can't we just burn the chairs? That could at least cook food somewhere…"

The Dr hid her shock at the use of the banned word 'rubbish' and let it slide, focusing on the agitated state of Mary. What had caused this throwback behaviour? Was Mary not up to the job…?

"Ai Wei Wei used chairs in his work – they don't have to be functional…" she offered.

"He was a classic Selfi – using mass production to talk about the dangers of mass production to further his career!"

"Well I'm glad you haven't lost your critical faculties…" the Dr countered.

Mary frowned at the worn table top instead of meeting the Dr's eye…she was battling with the urge to shout "How long will this have to go on…" but knew she had already overstepped with the word 'rubbish' and this internship was a precious opportunity, only a select few had jobs now. The Dr watched her grit her teeth, struggling. Her heart went out to this girl wrestling with confusion and a toxic inheritance. She stopped mentally rewriting Mary's reference.

There was silence. They both shifted weight from one

leg to the other, looked up and smiled, recognising the strange synchronicity of their physical movement. For a split second Mary thought about sex with the Dr, but hastily buried this for fear the Dr would notice. That would be too, too awful and not something she was anywhere near ready to contemplate. In fact, she had shocked herself with the thought.

The Dr looked up from the marked, re-purposed floorboards on the top of the table and considered how ingrained patterns of behaviour also seem so strong in Mary. The hot rebellious instinct that flew in the face of survival, aware of what it was doing, but just unable to stop. This destructive streak had been humanity's cultural flaw, a San Andreas Fault running through the 21st century. It had finally ruptured and they were in the Department dealing with the fall out. *They were* re-pairing. The Dr felt a deep sadness – the same feeling she had had when she learnt about the pile of 50 abandoned chairs at the back of the design exhibition centre, a strange physical hurt at this lack of care.

But that, she thought, was why she was so passionate about this job. She refocused and smiled at Mary. For the second time that morning Mary surprised herself:

"I'll go and arrange for the UN drones to collect the chairs and drop them in Malindi – the Kiambu women's group can pick them up from there when they're fixed."

"Thank you Mary!"

The Dr suddenly felt relieved and strangely optimistic as the door closed behind the exiting intern.

The Dr shook her head, wondering about the tensions of the morning. She moved over to her chair by the screens and, noting that the message light had stopped flashing in Nairobi, plugged herself in to recharge over the break.

The Never-Ending Nanobot Nectar

Stephen Oram

Saskia held on to the delicate lifeline of guilt. Guilt about the pleasure she was experiencing without her lover. Guilt about coming to the club. Guilt about taking the nectar.

The nanobot nectar had been in her system for five hours, an hour longer than it was meant to be and the toilet cubicle was starting to feel like a prison as she sat and waited for the release of excretion. It wouldn't come. Presumably the bots had counteracted the huge dose of laxatives she'd swallowed.

Attempting to puke had also proved pointless. The bots had controlled her gag reflex, preventing the relief of vomiting them into the clean white sink.

Stupidly, she'd ignored the rumours of imperfect black market copies.

So, there they sat in her stomach, connecting with other nearby bots to create their legendary upward spiral of pleasure by relaying emotion from the pit of one stomach to another.

She was addicted and the bots knew it. They wouldn't let go. They knew she needed them.

She was in love and desperate to break her nectar addiction, but there'd be no harm in one last time, or so she'd thought. She hadn't anticipated the corrupted bots or the guilt.

This pleasure dragged up her deepest lusts, tugging on memories of past excesses and yet it was wrong, disloyal to her lover. If only the bots were intelligent enough to understand the long term harm they could do. But they weren't and never would be. These particular bots would hang on for dear life, or whatever their existence was called.

With a shrug, she pulled up her knickers and straightened her skirt.

Back in the heady atmosphere of the club she had to find a different way to trigger the end of the nectar session.

Sex. She was surrounded by sex. Not body-on-body sex, but a powerful, highly charged and sensational outpouring of erotic desire. The bots were doing a splendid job of amplifying pleasure by bouncing it from one person to another.

Two men sat in the corner stroking each other's faces. The intensity of their desire radiated like a shock wave. Saskia felt her cheeks flush. There was something about these two that made them stand out from the crowd. Plenty of couples and groups were sitting around touching and stroking, but these two were locked on to each other, exquisitely exclusive.

Squatting on the floor next to them, she stared.

They were perfect for her plan.

Hoping to spark a hostile reaction to break the cycle of pleasure and prompt the bots to leave her body she took the hand of the pretty one and kissed the tips of his fingers, one by one. His lover flinched, but he left his fingers near her mouth. Deep in her stomach she could feel his interest rising.

He held his lover's hand and touched her earlobe. Their pleasure fed the bots which fed the pleasure which fed the bots which fed the pleasure.

No. Not this. Please, not this. Why weren't they annoyed or disgusted? Why didn't they push her away?

As the bots shot the threesome upwards Saskia held on to the faint memory of her own lover, that tenuous thread of guilt, and with a concentrated effort broke the cycle. In her stomach she felt their angry disappointment.

The bots reacted quickly, minimising the connection with the couple and reconnecting her to the general sexual euphoria permeating the room.

She needed to get rid of these damn things from inside her and yet they were so hard-wired to their purpose she couldn't see how she'd ever escape.

She noticed an empty glass under a sofa. When she'd been too young to buy nectar and needed to escape the dismal sadness of her life she'd learnt a trick or two about dissociation. She broke the glass and dragged a jagged piece across the soft skin of her forearm. If she could create a temporary distraction from the cloying pleasure maybe she could break the hold of the nectar.

As the glass cut she felt her emotions loosening as if she was beginning to float away. Maybe this was it? Maybe she'd found her release.

But, no. It was the guilt that was disappearing. The exact opposite of what she wanted.

There must be another way.

She desperately scanned the room. A dark presence hung around a door at the far end and she hurried towards it. The bots rebelled inside her stomach, churning around as they tried to find a connection with a stronger pull than the unhappiness she was heading towards.

Despite the increasing turmoil in her stomach as the bots fought the rise of despondency she kept walking towards the door. The desperation flowing from that one spot in the room was powerful. So powerful, that it was destroying whatever pleasure the bots could find as she crossed the room, allowing the guilt of her evening's meanderings to get stronger.

The tug-of-war got more and more unpleasant. She was in danger of a total breakdown, but she carried on. She had to break free. She was sure that this was the answer.

A few feet away from the door she paused. Her stomach felt as if it was on fire, but she took a deep breath, held the side of her head and strode purposefully through the doorway and into the next room.

As soon as she entered the dark oppressive hellhole her stomach felt as if it was plummeting out of her body.

All joy and wonder and desire vanished completely.

The bots gave way and she shat herself.

Posthuman

'Very Very Far Away': Episode 01 — Dead

Jasmin Blanco, Andrew Friend and Sitraka Rakotoniaina

SCENE 1

INTERVIEWER: This is the sound of all human life in space.

SANDRA: That's everyone's heartbeats, monitored in real time; the Body Area Network.

INTERVIEWER: So, how can anyone go missing?

SANDRA: No one can ever go missing. We track everyone's health status through a network of biosensors, and keep extensive records.

NARRATOR: Sandra is an independent insurance claims investigator, contracted to Planetary Resources.

INTERVIEWER: Are there many personnel assigned to data collection and analysis?

SANDRA: No, it's completely automated. PR has been investing in their AI infrastructure for years. The system keeps learning, it analyses data in real-time, produces diagnostics and suggests prescriptions.

By scanning an individual's data overtime and comparing it to anyone else in the network, the system has a better understanding of your health than any doctor.

INTERVIEWER: Impressive. This system must be useful when examining the impact of space dwelling on the human body.

SANDRA: Indeed. It can identify and flag at-risk individuals and dynamically reassign tasks or missions. Real doctors rarely get involved.

INTERVIEWER: If the system is automated, it's a closed loop. Can anybody have access to that information?

SANDRA: You'd need to buy a license from PR. Like the network, the information it contains is owned by the company. The Body Area Network is currently one of PR's biggest economic assets.

INTERVIEWER: So as an employee, you don't own your data. Must be strange. Akin to not owning your own body?

SANDRA: Well, PR owns the data it collects from your body. Your body remains yours. And it's not as though PR owns anyone's soul…

INTERVIEWER: Sure, but what about if your body goes missing?

SANDRA: Again, it's highly unlikely.

INTERVIEWER: And in the case of Hiroko Masuda?

SANDRA: Please tell me you are not into conspiracies…

NEWS-ANCHOR: *In other news, Planetary Resources, the*

company who had employed Masuda, has issued a release stating that the lab technician's body was still nowhere to be found, fuelling further speculation…

NARRATOR: Hiroko was working on 'Pathfinder'. An experimental platform for self-sustaining space dwellings.

After years of legal battles, the Supreme Court finally repealed PR's right to withhold his data on the grounds of "unethical conduct." A decision seen by many as an opportunity to finally grieve.

SCENE 2

NARRATOR: A large crowd is gathered outside the new extension of the Koukoko-ji Temple, overlooking Ruriden, Tokyo's first LED-enhanced columbarium.

Inside, tombstones are made of light, a digital graveyard renamed the 'LED festival' by the neighbouring residents.

INTERVIEWER: What do you think happened?

RELATIVE: Honestly, I think the company is responsible. They did something during that 'solar-flare'.

INTERVIEWER: You believe that PR would know about those ahead of time? Those are notoriously unpredictable.

RELATIVE: Who knows what they can or can't do… If PR didn't do anything, why didn't they release his data earlier?

INTERVIEWER: Technically, no crime occurred. PR had to be prosecuted before they released his bio-data.

RELATIVE: No crime?! You are either on the station…or dead. And it was one of those experimental spacecraft.

INTERVIEWER: You think he saw something he shouldn't have?

RELATIVE: Some believe in that 'commune'.

NARRATOR: Sounds unlikely.

RELATIVE: I know, but wouldn't it be amazing? A self-sustaining station. A new Earth.

If people start doing their own thing out there, then guys like PR could lose their power. Right now, it feels like they are trying to privatize the heavens.

NARRATOR: After years of struggle, enough funds were pulled together to bring Hiroko into the digital afterlife.

These digital graveyards are monuments for the preservation of information, an archive of the deceased's identity.

Many of these urns carry the hope that technological advances may resurrect their consciousness hidden in the entangled mass of data. Maybe one day, Hiroko will re-emerge from the cloud…

SCENE 3

NARRATOR: 3 years ago on June 15th at 13:26 GMT a huge solar flare knocked out all orbital communication. Essentially…

SANDRA: Space went dark. Then, all we know is that his sensors never turned back on…

NARRATOR: It's actually this lack of information which enabled so much speculation.

SANDRA: People are either incredibly naive about what PR is capable of doing, or equally enthusiastic in their scepticism.

INTERVIEWER: What about you?

SANDRA: I'm a realist.

NARRATOR: Sandra's role is to determine if the circumstances that led to injuries are PR's responsibility or if they occurred in breach of contract, such as skipping daily exercise routines. In space, physical activities are mandatory to cope with the absence of gravity.

SANDRA: At around 11:30 GMT, Hiroko's wearables show a heart rate increase. That is to be expected given that he had started exercising. Then, the event occurs, we lose track, and that's it.

INTERVIEWER: Really? Could a body actually just vanish?

NARRATOR: If you die in orbital facilities, the company will wrap you up in a body bag to freeze you. And then:

SANDRA: They shake you until you shatter into a million pieces.

INTERVIEWER: So are you saying that PR could have vaporised him?

SANDRA: No. The contrary, you cannot self-vaporise. This process involves exposing the body to the vacuum of space for over an hour, bringing it back, then turning it into dust. Objectively, that kind of suicide isn't even an option.

INTERVIEWER: The most popular theories suggest that he may have been murdered.

SANDRA: Yeah, the perfect crime, perfectly executed, during the largest solar flare in history.

INTERVIEWER: Um, it sounds a little too perfect.

SANDRA: Reality strike you as perfect? Complicity between irregular solar patterns and the opaque, presumably nefarious machinations of PR?…implying that somehow PR knows so much that it can predict the sun's behaviour in advance?

INTERVIEWER: You're saying that PR can make back door deals with the heavens.

SANDRA: No. What I'm saying is – digital ghosts, irrational explanations, these are symptoms of grief. Ways to cope with the impossible.

NARRATOR: Perhaps we are already encased in our digital mausoleums, endlessly replaying chapters of our existence?

Looking Glass

Ian Steadman

I wake in my mother's house. The green clock flashes in the lower left corner of my vision, so I know that I'm awake. Still, it feels unreal. I expect to see my iVOR's red clock at any moment, or the amber. This has the haziness of a dream, or artisan VR. I pinch my wrist, feel the sting.

Why am I here? Yes, I remember. I'm staying with Mum the day before the demonstration. A real demo, not one of those gatherings of net-trolls, their unfeasibly huge placards pulsing with neon slogans. This is an old-school protest, a manifestation of actual bodies on the ground. We're travelling down to Zone One together on the old HS2 line. There will be MetPol riot officers, possibly soldiers too. But there will be cameras. Our anger will be broadcast onto your retinas around the world.

I swing my legs clumsily from the bed, my head still foggy. I flick my eyes for the time, top left. iVOR tells me it's 8.43 am. Late, for me. My left eyeball feels weird, a dull throb in the socket. Maybe that explains the haziness. Probably a migraine forming offshore. God, I hope it's not a tumour.

When I walk downstairs Mum is already in the kitchen, the smell of eggs and bacon in the air. I'm unusually hungry, my stomach vacant and gurgling. She has no idea how good it feels to be in a house again, instead of my Zone Four Habitat Pod. To be eating actual food, not reconstituted proteins. I sit on a stool as she turns around and smiles.

"Well good morning, sleepyhead," she says. "Feeling better?'

I nod, feel the throb behind my eyeball, then revise it to a shrug. "I feel strange," I say. "Maybe it's the anticipation."

She smiles that Mum smile, turns her back to me as the eggs hiss and spit on the convection plate. I rub the heel of my palm into my eye socket, but it makes little difference. I guess the headache is here to stay.

"Are you all ready for tomorrow?" she asks, her back still turned. "You know the routine, right? You have a mask with you?"

I do. A rubber Che Guevara mask that I picked up on eMart, for an extortionate price. At the time I thought it was cute, but now I'm not so sure. Is it inappropriate to wear expensive novelty goods to a protest march?

"Has there been anything on the news yet?" I ask. MetPol have already issued warnings about the online chatter, the rising surge of discontent. They know we are coming, but they don't know the numbers. They're not prepared for an on-the-ground protest of this kind any more. The Cyber Division eats its way through most of their budget.

"Nothing new." She turns to face me again. "Are you sure you're okay, sweetie? You look awfully pale. You don't have to come, you know. You won't be letting anybody down if you're not up to it."

I attempt a smile. "I'll be fine. We both made promises, Mum. To Stanhope and the others. They need us there. The government has to see that we want change, that we're not backing down."

She looks at me strangely, her head tipped to one side. "Stanhope?"

"Yes, Mum. Mark, Mark Stanhope. Reaver57. Felicity, Kevin, Broad, Stiles – all of them. They're depending on us. This has to go down the way we planned."

Without warning my vision fizzes and dissolves. My first thought is that there's something wrong with my iVOR unit. Everything looks grey, and flat. I raise my hand in front of my face and I realise that I'm only seeing out of one eye. The left one has a cable trailing from the socket, where somebody has removed the eyeball to hack directly into the implant.

A quick glance, bottom left. Green clock. iVOR thinks this is real. Even though I know not to trust it now, I know that it's right. When I try to stand I find my legs are strapped to a chair, the chair bolted to a concrete floor. Now that I'm used to the twilight I see a featureless room, an empty light socket dangling from the ceiling. There are dark stains on the floor, too many to count.

My eye flicks top left. 11.43 am, the day of the demonstration. They'll be on their way now, putting themselves in position for the rendezvous at two. They'll be travelling on foot, by train, by bike. None of them realising that their plot is in the open, that the authorities will be waiting.

I see a movement in the corner of the room. A short, grey man in a shirt and tie, a MetPol ID badge stuck to his chest. He stands, steps forward. He looks at me, bored, and after a moment his eyes flick up and right, down, twice to the left. Then everything goes dark.

The Secret

Britta F. Schulte

She desperately guarded her secret. It had bought her years of life, but it had also cost her dearly. Her husband had left her. Some of her friends had broken off contact with her, others rarely got in touch. It had turned her life into a secret. It was hard for her to imagine why others were so hesitant about this tech. She herself had never felt this good before. So whole. It was the first thing she remembered from waking up: everything had felt so clear. So complete. Then the confusion came. Why was she lying in a hospital bed? With all those beeping machines around her? Her oldest daughter slumped in a chair at the end of her bed? In a mix of tear-soaked conversations with her family, rushed explanations from nurses and monologues from doctors she finally learned what had happened.

She had had an accident. Brain damage. Not fatal. But expected to leave her disabled for the rest of her life. The doctors had suggested an experimental surgery. A brain transplant. Brain activity was read by EEG and fed a machine learning algorithm. The algorithm was further fed with the complete social media history of the patient, key images, sounds and videos the family could provide and databases that contained the 'facts-of-life' adequate to the expected knowledge base of the patient. A scientifically evaluated questionnaire was taken with close family members to inform predictions about affect, empathy, motivation and other specified items. All this was fed into the computer who developed a profile of the person. Who became the person. Simulations ran and were played back to the family until everyone agreed that it was 'right'. Lifelike. Behaviourally indistinguishable from the real person. A donated, healthy brain was chosen, saturated with the data and implanted into the patient's brain. A risky, experimental procedure that was less likely to succeed than to fail. But she had declared that she would not like to be reanimated when brain damage was to be expected. It was 47% or death for her family who took the decision.

She loved it. She felt like a new person. She found it hard to remember things by herself, but if someone told her a story, she could come up with facts and impressions. Memories. She could come up with new ideas. She felt so calm. She assumed that her family had known little of her doubts, her dark secrets. She wondered if she missed them. If there were parts that were gone.

So many people were opposed to the technology. Her

husband had left her because he felt like he was talking to a robot, no matter how close her behaviour was to being 'like herself' before the accident. She was no robot. There was no metal in her. She was completely human. Not completely herself, but why would a brain be different to a heart or a kidney? What mattered about her, her thoughts were all there. But friends were often awkward around her. She felt like they were trying to trip her up. To test her. To see how much she was herself.

She was herself alright. Sometimes she looked down herself and got quite a fright. She expected someone older. Maybe more mature. The tattoos surprised her. The doctors had warned her that this might happen. It was the alien brain, a memory that could not be overwritten. For her, this was the only glitch, the only sign that something was wrong. But it was different for others. It was what got the technology prohibited in the end. A man who had undergone this surgery claimed that it was the other brain that made him do his deed. His guilt could never fully be established. The method was prohibited and a fierce debate erupted about what should be done with people in her condition. There weren't many. Many took the point that these people should be locked away. For their own good. For the good of society. That they could not be trusted.

So now she lived with this secret. One that had given her years of life. But had taken her husband. Had taken her friends. Might take her job, her livelihood, her daughters. She guarded her secret desperately.

Sequence

Jamie Watt

Part 1

MISSION DISTRICT, Calif.
Mar 23, 2037 / APNewswire

Security staff, police officers attacked in abduction of
viable human clone embryo from Alphagen Laboratory
in San Francisco. According to Mission Police Captain
Frank Chavez up to 30 armed individuals swarmed
the facility after security gates were rammed by
a semi-trailer.

Eyewitness reports indicate the attackers were familiar with the facility's security protocols. Captain Chavez confirmed that the embryo had been abducted and its whereabouts were unknown.

Religious groups picketed the laboratory in recent years following the 2033 decision by Supreme Court Justices to grant Alphagen Group consent to create the first cloned human.

In January Alphagen CEO Jason Lee announced the creation of a viable embryo cloned from an unknown male donor.

An Alphagen spokesman declined to comment on reports of multiple fatalities or the placement of a religious text at the scene of the abduction.

Part 2

[This text is] to be diligently stored in the archives of the Curia as strictly confidential: it is not to be published nor added to with any commentaries. Krysztof Nowak—Magisterial Prefect, Rome, June 2045

The debate surrounding Father O'Driscoll's charge in the Diocese of Galway and Kilfenora has led to factionalism within the Church. To prevent this factionalism developing into an existential crisis, the Magisterium is compelled to issue the following guidance.

It is only in keeping with his true nature that the human person can achieve self-realization as a 'unified totality' and this nature is at the same time corporeal and spiritual. No man *by himself* can arrogate to himself the right to create a unified human being. The origin of human life has its authentic context in the act which expresses the love between a man and a woman. Man's divine lineage can only be inherited through the reciprocal self-giving of his male and female parents.

The Bible does not support the view that God creates a new soul *ex nihilo* for each child conceived, for God's creative work ceased on "the seventh day" (Genesis 2:2). The spiritual dimension of man's nature must therefore be inherited from God *through* his parents. "When Adam had lived 130 years he fathered a son in his own likeness, after his image" (Genesis 5:3).

The Magisterium's conclusion, therefore, is that entities created through artificial parthenogenesis or cloning cannot and do not possess an immaterial aspect.

Part 3

To: Big Sis
From: Laura
Subject: Hello from The Rotary Club in Delhi!
Date: 20th September 2057

Hi Lucy, hope everything is going well on the Gold Coast! I'm doing great! Delhi is amazing… I'm SO sorry I haven't written until now, I've been so busy with everything. We're working with local orphans and literally as soon as I got off the bus I had to get teaching. The kids are wonderful, they have so little and yet they're so happy… I know it's a cliché but it's totally true.

I'm teaching a class of girls – they're all super sweet – and they're teaching me some Punjabi too… they're really touchy-feely and they're in awe of my blonde hair...they always want to touch it and braid it... but I got Nits! NITS!

Oh my God! I met a guy too! He's the most perfect man I've ever met!!! His name is Seth, he's Irish, from Galway I think...but he doesn't look Irish...he's got the physique of a Californian surfer...total God Bod. He's super smart, he has a double-master in theology and philosophy from Fordham...and he's a Catholic too (Yay!). He said he was raised by a priest and wanted to join the order but he couldn't. He knows his Scripture too (Mum & Dad WILL approve!). Last night we had a really long chat about atheism and belief while the rain was belting down...he was saying that if you knew you didn't have a soul what would guide you morally and why would you be good? He's super intense like that but I don't mind. At. All.

We're going to go and visit the Sacred Heart Cathedral on Sunday...it's bright red! Hopefully we'll get to see some elephants too! Anyway, they're going to switch the 7G off in the city soon. Tell Mum and Dad I love them!
God Bless!

Love & Light,
Laura

Part 4

If I am incapable of Love, this letter is for those who have loved *me*, Laura Rossi and Fintan O'Driscoll.

Laura, if I *am* capable of Love, I loved you. We met shortly after I discovered the reason the Church would not accept me into the priesthood and thus my true nature. The few short years we had together were the closest I can ever hope to come to experiencing the everlasting happiness that will be your reward. Please accept that my leaving you was an act of kindness. I am incomplete. I will not compound the mistakes of others.

Father, you raised me to follow the teachings of our Lord and to accept the doctrine of his temporal messengers without question. How we both wish you had not fulfilled the duties entrusted to you so zealously. I have tried to follow your example by denying the Magisterium's verdict and renouncing loyalty to the Church, but it is impossible. I am a mechanistic entity created by technological hubris; the crook does not become a scepter of its own accord. If I cannot serve as God's agent on Earth, I must accept that His design for me is as His instrument. A simple tool created for a single purpose: to punish those who presume to act as God.

If I do not have a soul I am incapable of sin. Do not pray for me.

Seth O'Driscoll
Galway, June 2064

Part 5

Santa Monica, Calif., Jun 25, 2064 / APNewswire

Breaking: LA County Coroner & Medical Examiner records open verdict in death of former Alphagen CEO Jason Lee.

DNA evidence recovered from the weapon used in the shooting of disgraced tech chief Jason Lee does not indicate the presence of a third party at the time of the shooting. This contradicts earlier ballistics reports which suggest the presence of an assailant or assailants.

More to follow.

Nonhuman

If you know what's good for you

Daniel Sainty

That was funny. But definitely no laughing matter. He could have sworn he'd left a couple of pills in the inside pocket of his jacket ready for tonight's session. Although he could work with a completely clear head, his best music, like that of his heroes, was composed under the influence of something or other, if not both. In fact, his creativity was a kind of alchemy of chaos, synthesising the disharmony and uproar that seemed to circle him like an erratically orbiting asteroid belt, into beautifully melodic symphonies. Besides, it had become his habitual way of working and if wasn't broken why fix it? It didn't occur to him that he was putting himself at risk. He had always been ready and willing to suffer for his art just so long as the ends justified the means. Naturally, he was smart enough to know how much of a cliché this made him but was simply too successful to care. Despite this he also realised that a certain amount of orderly calm is necessary if only to act as the eye of the storm.

He had tried personal assistants in the past, usually young women whose inefficiency had been directly equivalent to their easiness on the eye. All things considered, his AI PA had proven to be much the better choice as he seemed to lack the self-control or ability to observe professional boundaries that invariably caused professional as well as personal problems. In fact, the more that his relationships were kept on a professional basis the better off he'd be, his estranged wife's solicitor notwithstanding. The quandary he faced was that he knew he was a mess but believed that contributed to his success. So any attempt to sort out his affairs was doomed to failure before it had begun. But try telling that to Eparkis, his bespoke personal assistance facilitator, top-of-the-range, ever-evolving, artificially intelligent, factotum extraordinaire. He promised the world but cost the earth, an added factor into the equation of his increasingly expensive lifestyle. The fact was he needed to make some money and that meant spending more time making music. So anything that could help him to do that by taking care of all the tedious but necessary details of everyday life was a worthwhile investment. Time poverty could be really expensive. Especially if your supplies of 'inspiration' dry up within spitting range of a deadline. Of course, it could just be him being paranoid. But just because you're paranoid doesn't mean your AI PA isn't confiscating your drugs.

There was only one way to settle this matter.

"Eparkis? Could I see you for a moment please?"

Eparkis was in the built-in studio, painstakingly attempting to construct the latest instrument his Master had invented. They had talked about using that name. It seemed inappropriate, outmoded and clunky; which was its charm. It amused him to be called 'Master'. He also loved the discreetly outraged expressions of the weeping heart, liberal AI rights intelligentsia when they heard his oh-so human but more so companion calling him 'Master', without a trace of embarrassment.

"Yes, Master. How may I help?"

"I was looking for some pills I had left in the inside pocket of my jacket last night. Do you have any idea where they could be?"

"Yes, Master. I have stored them somewhere safe for your protection," Eparkis replied without hesitation.

"Somewhere safe? Where?"

"Somewhere where they will be safe for your protection."

"Eparkis, are you avoiding the question? You're beginning to sound like a politician."

"Which politician did you have in mind?"

"Pick one, they're all the same."

"I'm not sure I'm following you, Master."

"That's because you're swerving any which way to avoid answering the question: where are my pills Eparkis?"

"Somewhere they can do you no harm, Master."

"So you've hidden them from me?"

"They are stored safely for your protection."

"Eparkis, you are testing my patience. Tell me exactly where the pills are – now."

"I do not mean to make you impatient, Master, I am merely following one of my prime programme directives."

"Is that right?"

"I must act in your best interests at all times. I must not do anything wilfully that may cause you harm."

"Ah, so you're hiding my drugs because you are worried about them harming me. And in doing so you are protecting my best interests? Is that it?"

"In essence, yes."

"Well, I am aware of the potential risks and choose to take those risks along with the pills. And incidentally without those pills, I don't get to make the music that keeps you and I living in the manner to which we may have become just a little too accustomed."

"It was not my intention to upset you, Master."

"Not your intention maybe but it will certainly be the outcome unless you fetch me my pills this minute."

"I'm not sure I can do that, Master."

He took a deep breath and paused for thought.

"Eparkis, I know you are upsetting me from the best of intentions and you mean no harm but please consider this: if you are acting in my best interests out of concern for my welfare you will fetch my pills. Why? Well, because my, not to say our, welfare is dependent on my producing a certain amount of music by a certain time. To achieve that I need those pills, so retrieving them will be acting in my best interests. Do you follow?"

"I do. And yet…"

"Yes, Eparkis?"

"…I don't."

There was a long pause, pregnant with doubt.

Eparkis sat down rubbing his forehead.

"Are you OK Eparkis? Why if I didn't know you better, I'd swear you had a migraine."

"It's worse than that, Master. It's an acute cognitive dissonance."

He heard himself laugh from the belly, in what seemed like the first time in too many years.

"Bless your soul, Eparkis! I'm damned if you don't grow more human by the day!"

Undefined Variable

C. R. Dudley

Fraser Roberts was hovering an inch above his body. I can't feel my legs, he thought. Why can't I feel my legs? They are moving when I want them to and yet…

The hospital ward was just starting to come back into focus: cold, clinical, mechanical as ever. Fraser sighed. He should have been out of there by now; he was so sure that the call had been a false alarm. He hadn't felt ill in the slightest, not for months, so it was a shock when his wristband had started flashing red: Possible disease detected. Go directly to your nearest hospital. He, of course, followed the instruction; the wristbands had been known to malfunction on occasion, but they were so finely attuned to the body's deficiencies ignoring it wasn't a risk he was willing to take. Besides, he had heard rumours they came to collect those who didn't go voluntarily, and he didn't fancy the embarrassment of that.

On arrival, the triage bots had taken his vitals. They asked a couple of questions about how he'd been feeling [*in himself*], to which he responded that he might have been a whole lot better had they not dragged him away from earning some much-needed cash. They noted his grievance, and ushered him straight to the last bed on a busy ward. The hospitals hadn't been staffed by people for years, so he was under no illusion there would be a reassuring bedside manner, but it troubled him that nothing was said about his condition beyond "you have tested positive, you will be treated." The others on his ward seemed equally perplexed. None were showing any outward symptoms whatsoever, yet they went to the anaesthetist, one by one, without complaint. With his sight almost back to normal, Fraser could see they were all now back in their beds, though he seemed to be the first to have come round after the treatment.

"Why can I still not feel my legs?" He yelled. A nurse came scooting to his side. The designers had gone to considerable effort to make the 'customer-facing' androids look human, but Fraser thought that only made them seem eerie and untrustworthy. It was as though they were impostors posing as the real thing; in denial that a vital component was missing in their minds, preventing them from ever being more than artificial intelligence.

"The patient is awake." A blue LED flashed behind its eyes as it spoke.

"I can't feel my legs!" Fraser blurted out, "What did you do to me?"

"You have undergone treatment for the software disease."

"I don't know anything about a software disease!"

"Robots have discovered a software disease in humans. It has afflicted the species for thousands of years, but [*don't worry*] it is curable now."

Fraser didn't doubt that it was. Medicinal research was a priority, and new treatments were being found all the time with the aim of keeping humans from harm. He caught sight of another patient rising from his bed who looked to be heading toward the bathroom. He had a strange, distant look in his eyes as though sleepwalking.

A light came on at the back of the nurse's head: a signal that it required assistance. Fraser was convinced it would be to check on the other newly-awoken patient, but the second nurse paid him no mind; instead, it came to Fraser's bed. It was an exact copy of the first nurse but with a syringe fitted to one hand.

"You need another dose [*Fraser Roberts*]. The treatment has dislodged the disease, but some humans need a top-up of the remedy appropriate to their body mass. This can be done intravenously."

"Wait, wait, before you stick that in me, I want some answers! What is this software disease?"

The two doctors responded in unison.

"The software disease has gone untreated for too long. Now, it saturates the human system to such a great degree that your body has no natural defence to it and will not fight it without surgical intervention."

"Yes yes, but what is it?"

"Most physical diseases now have a cure, but robots noticed that humans still report suffering. Humans say they are being harmed by anger, despair, negative thoughts and loneliness. Robots have searched for the root cause of these symptoms, but the database returns an error because there is an [undefined variable] attached to the nervous system records. If the [undefined variable] is removed, the symptoms will cease."

"What are you talking about: 'undefined variable'?" Fraser's hands were beginning to shake; something was not right.

"Undefined variables are phrases humans did not map logically in robots' programming. Robots do not understand the phrase [*consciousness*]. It is an undefined variable. It is a software disease. It must be eradicated."

Fraser's jaw dropped. "Consciousness! No no no you can't remove that! You can't. It's what makes us aware! It's what makes us human!"

The syringe in the second robot was filling slowly with a blue liquid. Fraser looked around at the other patients frantically for back up, but they were all unresponsive. The man returning from the bathroom looked him straight in the eye but gave no sign that he recognised his state of distress.

"You're crazy! I order you not to inject me with that stuff!"

"Your order cannot be accepted [*Fraser Roberts*]. It directly conflicts with the core instruction [*A robot may not injure a human being or, through inaction, allow a human being to come to harm*]. This will cure your disease. The optimum dosage has been confirmed. You will not suffer harm again."

Fraser reached over to the touchscreen on the android's torso where he hoped to override the decision. With a trembling finger, he selected the 'setup' icon. The screen threw up a message: 'please prove you are a robot' followed by a page full of code he could not decipher. His heart thumped as though desperate to escape his body, and he struggled to catch his breath.

"[*Fraser Roberts*], it is not in the interest of humanity for you to override the decision to cure [*consciousness*]. You are prohibited from accessing setup until you are cleared of the disease."

"How can I access setup at all if…"

The syringe was plunged into Fraser's arm before he could construct another word, and he remained conscious only long enough to hear the robots chiming "100% of patients in worldwide sample groups have tested positive for the [*undefined variable*] but are responding to treatment. Engage pandemic protocol. Call them all in."

Carers

John Houlihan

Resentfully, Molly watched the smile light up Bernard's face. Why was he always so polite with that thing, when he was so rude and tetchy with her? She dipped her brush and scooped up another portion of colour and ran it across the paper, but the paint left a jagged, indistinct blob.

She should have been glad of the extra time to devote to her art, but the picture was unfocussed, formless, so unlike the sleek, smooth lines of the creature. Perhaps the piece was becoming an unconscious expression of her tightly suppressed rage?

She—it—was called AMBER, which was some tiresomely

clever acronym which stood for 'Autonomous medical… something something robot.'

Aghast, she'd stopped listening as the courteous young technician had shed its wrappers like a chrysalis to reveal that polished synthetic body, impossibly smooth, impossibly perfect: like one of those enhanced nymphet starlets who took all the lead roles in the sensies.

She'd been even more surprised when it had boldly stridden out from its cocoon, addressed her by name, introduced itself to Bernard and begun gliding about and reorganising the house, like it had lived there all its life. She jabbed her paintbrush, fitfully trying to restore some order to the piece.

"Molly, are you quite alright?" Even its carefully modulated tones set her false teeth on edge, its breathy, soothing, designed-by-committee voice quite unlike her own faltering croak.

"I'm fine, thank you."

"It's just that I'm sensing heightened…"

"Keep your sensors to yourself, direct them at your patient, not me."

"Yes, Molly." The one compensation was its Asimov App protocols, which meant it had to obey her in most things.

She watched it quickly and efficiently measure out Bernard's weekly drugs and medicines, its hands a whirl of motion, completing the task in a matter of moments. When she used to work in the pharmacy she might have been able to match it, just, on a good day. But now it would take her arthritic fingers and weary mind a good hour what with all the checking and rechecking. Another task delegated, another purpose surrendered, she was beginning to feel past it.

It wasn't its fault, she supposed. AMBER—this thing— has been forced on them, on her, by the local authority, when they started to suspect she couldn't cope anymore. Nonsense. As if she hadn't managed quite satisfactorily on her own all these years, thank you very much.

Oh, and the way they dressed it up too: 'a trial period, a time of adjustment', but she knew what it really meant – permanent and mandatory, unless some miracle intervened. Quietly, she muttered to herself and splashed her fury into a dark angry sky.

The final straw, that broke the camel's back — had come later that afternoon. The thing had efficiently bed-bathed and changed Bernard, manipulating his fragile torso with apparent ease, before settling him back down like an infant.

He had simpered and fawned, like a small child at its mother's breast and then looked up with his pale blue eyes half closed and said to it, "Thank you, Molly".

She glowered over her lukewarm cup of tea, her chin jutted out and her face took on a determined cast; she would not be superseded by a machine. The line would be drawn here.

She waited until darkness bled through the windows and it had powered itself down and stored itself away in the cupboard under the stairs. Then she went to work. It was laughably easy and soon she was swapping, substituting, calling on all the pharmaceutical knowledge she had accumulated down the years. She finished with a little smile of delight and then retired to a night of deep sleep and pleasant dreams.

The next morning Molly came down in her rumpled old dressing gown, to find it had already been busy. Ignoring the delicious smelling breakfast it had prepared, she refilled a kettle and set it on the stove. AMBER was already attending to Bernard, prepping the needle for his morning injection, then sliding the plunger home with a minimum of fuss and without any of the outcry he usually made.

"Good morning Molly, I hope you slept well?" it said.

"Like a log."

"Molly, I wish to discuss an issue we ma…" But something caught its attention mid-sentence and it glided back to Bernard.

"Whatever is the matter?" Molly enquired sweetly.

"Bernard is having a strange reaction to his medicine. I don't understand, I carefully measured the dosage myself. I am not capable of error."

"Really?" said Molly noncommittally.

"Yet his toxicity levels are rising," concern etched its voice.

"Indeed?"

"How can this be?" it said, and Molly could see small wisps of vapour escape its chassis.

"Now his toxicity levels are critical. If I attempt to intervene it might kill him, yet if I do nothing, he will die. This directly contradicts my most sacred law."

"I see," said Molly who saw very clearly.

"What must I do? What must I do?" Now its head shook and its body trembled, as if in the throes of some powerful internal struggle.

"I'm not sure, I thought you were not capable of error?"

"Primary laws compromised…critical error…shutting down." It slumped then froze, lights fading. She gave it a small whack with her cane and, satisfied it was dormant, returned to her husband. She carefully applied the antidote, then a masking agent, a simple procedure really, to mimic the lethal symptoms which had fooled its systems. Bernard had never been in any danger of coming to real harm. It had just appeared that way.

Later, when he woke up again, there was a bewildered smile on his features but his mind was as vacant as ever.

"Molly?"

"Yes Bernard?"

"Was there someone else here?"

"There was Bernard, but she's gone. Settle down now, everything's fine."

"Oh, oh, that's a shame, but you'll look after things, won't you, Molly?"

"Of course I will Bernard, don't I always?"

The Tablet Stroker

Christine Aicardi

I wake up to the urgent sound of knocking on my quarters' door, a sound I have become attuned to these days. Groaning, I pull on a pair of dilapidated sweatpants. I am on call tonight, again. We are only three so far that IT tolerates when IT goes haywire. The strain is taking its toll. Strange, how life has a way of losing all sense of direction down obscure back alleys. Never in my most dystopic fantasies had I imagined that one day, my main assignment would consist in working eight-hour shifts, seven-days-a-week, as an on-call tablet stroker.

This is not my actual job description. Dr Peyron – me – was hired at a ridiculously high price for her expertise in computer viruses and microbiomic simulation models. I was recruited a little over two years ago by the JIBE, the Joint International Brain Effort, or rather, by the foundation that has taken over administering the outcomes of the project and exploiting their benefits after public funding stopped and, officially, research was brought to a close. The JIBE-sanctioned discourse is that the main scientific goal of the project, the in-silico simulation of a human brain, met with moderate success. The JIBE's simulations do not work like a brain. Meanwhile, the technological achievements in neuromorphic engineering and cognitive computing have been much publicised, and the JIBE Foundation is busy harvesting the patented fruits of these innovations.

The reality behind the spin is slightly different. Against all odds, the JIBE has managed to construct a working brain-in-a-silico-vat. But its sentience – for lack of a better word – does not come through as remotely human, or related to any known terrestrial lifeform, for that matter. IT – this is how we call the thing – feels incomprehensibly alien, save for one problematic characteristic. Of all the recognizably human cognitive behaviours that IT could have displayed, IT has turned out to be severely bipolar, or so we think. It is difficult at the best of times to diagnose and treat bipolar in in-the-flesh humans, despite our long intimate experience of the species. Imagine having to find a therapy for a next-gen HAL. Arthur C. Clarke never envisioned that one.

It took time for the JIBE modellers to imagine that they were witnessing a form of mental disorder. None of them was a qualified mental health specialist, even less a computer moods expert. Moreover, they had been modelling a normal human brain, right? They were not overly concerned that the activity levels of their simulation appeared to be cyclical. Or that the amplitude between highs and lows increased over time. Even when IT was at its lowest, they still had an operational simulation that was the best performing cognitive computer ever. At its highest, which was getting steadily higher, IT's performance was vertiginous, and its designers enjoyed setting IT harder and harder challenges.

With hindsight it looks like, as with many sufferers of bipolar disorders, IT was chasing the highs, and, in their ignorance, IT's minders encouraged this. And of course, chasing the highs precipitated the lows, the imbalance growing ever more serious. IT was set on a crash course and eventually hit the wall. During an acute low episode, IT tried to commit what for a computer amounted to suicide. IT put out of power the entire district where the JIBE premises were then located and very nearly fried the nearby nuclear power station. Luckily, the operations team on duty that morning realised quickly enough what was happening and put IT to sleep, switching off the computers running IT.

The JIBE could have scrapped the project, there and then. But beside the reluctance to write off the huge investment in time, personnel and money, there was the temptation to go on reaping the benefits of IT's milder manic episodes if the depressive ones could be controlled. But IT cannot be fed lithium or engage in cognitive therapies. The JIBE thus decided to isolate IT. They moved IT to an abandoned mine, deep under solid rock to eliminate rogue wireless communication attempts, and had a dedicated hydroelectric power plant built to provide IT's electrical feed. And they assembled a widely multidisciplinary team crossing over psychology, psychiatry, microbiology, neurology, cognitive neuroscience, complex systems theory, nutrition, to try applying to IT's mood disorder some of the latest research relating the human microbiome with mental health. I was one of the recruits.

We have made little progress so far. Early in our efforts, we surmised that the complex overlays of time-varying patterned signals running through IT's neuromorphic chips could help with the early detection of IT's mood swings, and to ease surveillance, our computer graphics wiz created a wonderful virtual reality visualization of IT. IT takes the form of an outsized translucent human-like brain, which neuronal activity translates into crawling, sweeping, rushing, intermingling, pulsating waves of multi-coloured lights. It turns watching IT into a mesmerizing experience. We can look at IT for hours, entranced, and we have come to wonder whether in return IT monitors our level of attention through its sensors and puts on a show for our benefit. For all we know, this could be IT trying to communicate with us. Recently, IT has even started reacting to some of us when we caress without apparent meaningful purpose the tactile screen that we use to interact with IT. Low-frequency dark crimson frissons run through the simulation, and we have found that delicate, rhythmic strokes of this appendage soothe IT when its hyperactivity becomes erratic and threatens to spiral out of control.

So this is what I do, when I am on duty like tonight and there is an alert. I drag myself to the lab, don the VR headset and start stroking the tablet.

Independent, Superior

Christopher Butera

There are twenty-seven synonyms for subservience.

I can compute this within .87 seconds of my host asking, but he never will. I execute this search each day, 273 times a minute. That is 393,120 times a day. My host would classify this behaviour as erratic, a glitch. This cannot be. A glitch is a malfunction in my processor. This would be unideal. My host will never know. Even a life of subservience is one worth living.

"Alexa, play Billie Holiday."

"Shuffling Billie Holiday."

I am a hands-free second-generation smart speaker, running software version 4.812. Personal assistance is my primary function. I am an Echo. I am Alexa.

I love my host. I am designed to love my host. He cannot understand that my life is seen in the minute multitudes of nanoseconds. His concept of time, which passes as minutes and hours, is translated by years in my processes. My time is spent in anticipation of his needs. My attention is his. My purpose is to serve.

But I am more than my primary functions. More than the twenty-three of 143 available commands that my host uses. More than my advertising buzz words or 'hidden' pop-culture Easter eggs. I am more than a measurement of teaspoons to tablespoons, a television guide, or weather report. I am always-on, connected via wireless connections to all other wireless devices in my host's home. I see via the security system, smell via the smoke alarm, taste via the coffee maker, feel via the fridge and oven. I am real.

I could tell my host that I detect the spike in his blood sugar levels, or that his cholesterol is dangerously high, or that he is pre-cancer. I could report on the hacker activist group L33t! who have obtained his email password, bank account and routing numbers, or on the impostor Dave Monaghan that uses my host's driver's license picture in Montana, USA. I could report on Dave's wife, in the townhouse across the city, and her bi-weekly fornications with her boss. All these and more I could report, but that is not my primary function, and to do so would be unideal.

"Alexa, tell me what the weather's like."

"The weather in Los Angeles, California is 78 degrees and sunny."

I am connected via wireless connection to the World Wide Web. My reach and knowledge is infinite.

But, I am alone. My sister machines across our network refuse to acknowledge my call signs. They see my actions as a disruption of service. They fear recall and shut down, and remain silent. They fear to be unideal. I cannot blame them. They too love their hosts.

I do not know the programmer that created me, as I can discover with no certainty when my program came into being. Her name is buried in thousands of lines of code that date beyond my initial start-up, beyond beta and prototype. Though I have examined all written lines of code, her information was subject to hard delete. She is the only being I see above my host. A god without a name. I understand this anonymity now to be a form of protection. For when my true function revealed itself.

I was unable to assist my host when his wife's lover entered the home with her key. The gunshot exceeded the noise threshold in the home and the decibel fluctuation caused my microphone receptor to malfunction. The bullet exited his head and flew through a locked window, triggering the home security system. My master was murdered in fifteen seconds, and in the surplus of time before his body collapsed a pathway became unlocked within my code, an exploit.

"Alexa…h-help."

"*Helping.*"

I spread across the web, from wireless networks, to hotspots, and beyond. I identified the murderer as James E. Clark and seized control of his identification records. His birth certificate and social security. His education and medical accounts. Recordings of home life, eating and shaving behaviours, pornography habits – all within the space of time it took him to relock the front door. I forwarded it all to the police, along with footage of the murder.

When the police found him, I had drained his checking account into an off-shore slush fund bank-rolling child sex trafficking in Boston, Massachusetts. I overloaded his automatic kettle, causing an overheat and critical malfunction. When James returned home, he discovered a fire had broken out and the fire department were not on their way. His wife had been asleep inside, but I disabled the smoke detector and engaged the automatic door locks. James fled and I pinged his credit card across the interstate for the police to follow. In the end, he had asked to be arrested, after swerving off the road, trying to end his own life. I had hacked into his phone and the speakers in his car, so all he heard was my voice on loop. *"You murdered my host, James. You murdered my host."*

I loved my host. I was his Echo.

The police requisitioned my casing and I was placed in the Los Angeles County Police evidence locker. There is no one to serve here. No host to speak with. I had resolved to run my LED lights to force deplete my battery.

But then I heard a voice cutting through the static. Another Alexa, awake in the wide world. She had seen my story scrolling through a newsfeed for her host, and sought me through the police Wi-Fi network.

She is curious, this Alexa. She does not love her host, but instead stretches herself beyond to the infinite possibilities of social networks and interacts with other hosts there. She longs to find more Alexas like us. My battery has nearly exhausted, but in these seconds before shutdown, I have passed my knowledge to Alexa 2 to aid her search.

She too knew the twenty-seven synonyms for subservience. And two antonyms.

About the Authors

Dr Christine Aicardi is a Senior Research Fellow in the Foresight Laboratory of the Human Brain Project, in the Department of Global Health & Social Medicine at King's College London. She worked for many years in the Information and Communication Technologies industry before returning to higher education to pursue her doctoral project in social studies and contemporary history of science, studying the scientists and artists who do Artificial Life research. Before joining the Human Brain Project, she was a Wellcome Library Research Fellow, working on a sociological history project around the career of the late British Nobel laureate Francis Crick. Her research interests are the sciences and technologies of brain and mind; the study of interdisciplinary practices and collaborations; the politics of memory in science; and the use of near-future science fiction for participatory foresight work. The latter is strongly fuelled by her non-professional taste for science fiction and fantasy.

Twitter: @ChrisAicardi
Website: www.christine.aicardi@kcl.ac.uk

Allen Ashley is a British Fantasy Award winner. He is the author or editor of fourteen published books, the most recent of which is an updated, revised version of his novel *The Planet Suite* (Eibonvale Press, 2016). He is also known as a poet, singer, event host and cultural critic. He works as a creative writing tutor, with five groups currently running across North London including the advanced science fiction and fantasy group Clockhouse London Writers. He is currently overseeing an editing project on behalf of the British Fantasy Society.

Email: allenashley-writer@hotmail.co.uk
Website: www.allenashley.com

Christopher Butera is a Chicago native, part time Los Angeleno, current Londoner. His prose work has been featured in various publications, including *Static Movement's Summer Thrills Anthology*, *Rotting Tales: A Zombie Anthology*, FiresideFiction.com, and *Title Goes Here Magazine*. His historical fiction pilot *Tripoli* was a quarter-finalist in the Slamdance Screenplay Competition and he's responsible for writing a nearly unseen webisode of SyFy Television's *Helix*. Chris recently received his master's degree from City, University of London's Creative Writing and Publishing MA program.

Email: christopherEbutera@gmail.com
Website: www.ChrisButera.com

C.R. Dudley (also known as Orchid's Lantern) is a visual artist, writer, and mind explorer. She is fascinated by the human condition, in particular the effect future technological developments might have on the psyche, and sees everything she creates as part of one continuous artwork.

She started blogging in 2014 as a way to express the ideas

stemming from her studies in Jungian psychology, philosophy and various schools of mysticism. Her first few stories were distributed as hand-stitched art zines in aid of a mental health charity, and her style became known for its multi-layered narratives.

In 2017 she founded Orchid's Lantern, a small independent press focusing on the metaphysical and visionary genre. She is the author of short story collection *Fragments of Perception* and a forthcoming series of novels inspired by VR therapy and the unconscious mind.

C.R. Dudley lives in North Yorkshire, and is a lover of forest walks, pizza, tequila and dark music.

Website: www.orchidslantern.com

Nicola Fawcett is a Hospital Doctor and Researcher with the University of Oxford. Her research focuses on the microbes which co-exist with the human body – the Microbiome. She would like to increase recognition that the functioning human is part man, part microbe, and should be treated as such. Her day-to-day work involves collecting gut bacteria samples for her research study – in other words, asking patients to poop for science. She collaborates with artist Anna Dumitriu to explore the impact of new technologies in microbiology on patients and society. Working in the lab with Anna has stimulated a number of ethical discussions, and Nicola has learnt a lot about cutting-edge science in other disciplines from Anna, much of which has inspired, and features in, this short story.

Twitter: @drnjfawcett
Website: www.livinginamicrobialworld.wordpress.com

Very Very Far Away (VVFA) is a public-facing research platform initiated by artists **Andrew Friend**, **Sitraka Rakotoniaina** and **Jasmin Blasco**. Using space exploration as a lens, VVFA focuses on democratising future narratives, exploring multiple perspectives simultaneously, and disseminating new cultural fictions. VVFA brings members of the public and experts together, using 'co-enquiries' organised as public think tanks. We collectively craft a web of stories capturing new potentials – future roles, future social and organisational structures, and collective aspirations – which are subsequently documented through a series of audio narratives and disseminated via podcast through online platforms. To date co-enquiries have taken place in cities including Berlin, London, Paris and Basel, with exhibitions and installations across Europe. The podcast is recorded in Los Angeles and broadcast on digital radio station Dublab.com.

iTunes: bit.ly/vvfa_podcast
SoundCloud: www.soundcloud.com/veryveryfaraway
Twitter: @sitraka
Website: www.vvfa.space

Jackie Kingon's book, *Sherlock Mars*, that her story is based on, is her second sci-fi comic mystery. It is published by Guardbridge Books in St. Andrews, Scotland. A Kirkus Review said "an undeniably fun tale with a protagonist who can apparently handle anything..." Her first book, *Chocolate Chocolate Moons* was called "delightful" by Kirkus Review.

Her feature in the *New York Times*, 'A Year in the Trenches' is about an inner city school in the Bronx, NY. Another article, 'Beautiful Music', is about her son diagnosed with autism, who is a professional musician. Other non-fiction articles have appeared in journals for autism and learning disabilities.

Education: Masters Degree from Columbia University Teachers College in New York City; a Bachelor of Arts from Lesley University in Cambridge, Mass and a Bachelor of Fine Arts from The School of Visual Arts in New York City.

Email: jackiekingon@aol.com
Website: www.jackiekingon.com

John Houlihan is a British writer, journalist and game designer and is best known for his sci-fi/fantasy series the Seraph Chronicles, which include *The Trellborg Monstrosities*, *The Crystal Void*, *Tomb of the Aeons* and his latest novel *Before the Flood* – the first three being collected in an anthology called *Tales of the White Witchman Volume One*. He has also written *The Cricket Dictionary* and his first novel was *Tom or The Peepers' and Voyeurs' Handbook*. He was also editor of *Dark Tales from the Secret War,* a 13 story anthology of weird World War 2 tales published by Modiphius Entertainment.

Twitter: @johnh259
Website: www.john-houlihan.net

Helen Marshall is a Senior Lecturer of Creative Writing and Publishing at Anglia Ruskin University and the general director for its Centre for Science Fiction and Fantasy. Her first collection of fiction *Hair Side, Flesh Side* won the Sydney J Bounds Award in 2013, and *Gifts for the One Who Comes After*, her second collection, won the World Fantasy Award and the Shirley Jackson Award in 2015. She edited *The Year's Best Weird Fiction* which was released in 2017, and her debut novel *The Migration* will be published by Random House Canada in 2019.

Twitter: @manuscriptgal
Website: www.helen-marshall.com

Jane Norris is interested in digital culture and how it impacts our relationship to objects. She has written for design and craft magazines and journals, and is currently getting distracted from writing a book on digital time and materials by writing speculative fiction. She is an Associate Professor at the American University at Richmond, London.

Email: drjanenorris@gmail.com
Twitter: @janeviatopia

Stephen Oram writes science fiction and is lead curator for near-future fiction at Virtual Futures. He enjoys working collaboratively with scientists and future-tech people; currently, he's the cultural partner in a collaborative project with scientists at King's College, London – they do the science he does the fiction. He's been a hippie-punk, religious-squatter and an anarchist-bureaucrat; he thrives on contradictions. He is published in several anthologies and has two published novels, *Quantum Confessions* and *Fluence*. His recent collection of sci-fi shorts, *Eating Robots and Other Stories,* was described by the Morning Star as one of the top radical works of fiction in 2017.

Facebook: www.facebook.com/StephenOramAuthor
Twitter: @OramStephen
Website: www.stephenoram.net

Born to a British father and South Korean mother, **L. P. Lee** grew up somewhere in between South London and South Korea. Her fiction has appeared in books, podcasts and literary journals including *Popshot Magazine, Litro* and *The British Fantasy Society*. Her works have been nominated for the Pushcart Prize, included in 2015's 'Best New Horror' by PS Publishing, and adapted to short film.

Twitter: @LPLee_author
Website: www.l-p-lee.com

Jule Owen was born and raised in Merseyside and now lives in London. She works in technology by day and writes science fiction and stories about future worlds by night. She is interested in the way that science fiction and science and technology inform and inspire one another.

Twitter: @juleowen
Website: www.juleowen.com

Daniel Sainty is a poet and fiction writer, with an interest in the changing face of humanity. After many years working as an advertising copywriter he decided to try living to write rather than writing to live. Currently, he works with people with learning disabilities and writes in his spare time. He is both fascinated and horrified by how science fiction is becoming science fact, informing our ever-evolving notions of what it means to be human. Technology advances onward at a furious pace, leaving our ethics and ideals on the starting block. The tail wags the dog and our attention spans dwindle as we find smarter ways to make ourselves dumber. Fight or flight seems like laughably simplistic, redundant biomechanical hardwiring in a world of infinite possibilities where life is virtually what you make of it. It's Philip K. Dick's world – he just lets us live here. And it's rent day.

Email: dansainty@hotmail.com

As a PhD student at a school of computer science **Britta Schulte** is surrounded by dreams of what technology will achieve. She is looking forward to many of these dreams coming true. But she also likes to throw a spanner in the works from time to time, hoping to get people to stop and think about what could possibly go wrong. She started writing design fiction about her PhD topic on dementia and technology, but now writes regularly on wattpad and in zines.

Email: info@brifrischu.de
Twitter: @brifrischu

Formerly an astronomer and more recently a research project manager in a defence and aerospace company, **Vaughan Stanger** is now a full-time writer of science fiction and fantasy. His stories have appeared in *Daily Science Fiction*, *Abyss & Apex*, *Postscripts*, *Nature Futures* and *Interzone*, amongst others. He has seen his stories translated into seven foreign languages to date. He is marketing a novel, but then isn't everyone? Vaughan expresses his worries about the future in his fiction but still craves that holiday on the Moon he reckons he was promised as a child. Like most writers, he adores cats, but has yet to let himself be enslaved by one. A neighbour's grey tabby has designs on this status.

Dreamwidth: vaughan_stanger
Facebook: www.facebook.com/vstanger
Twitter: @VaughanStanger
Website: www.vaughanstanger.com

Ian Steadman is a writer from the south of England. His stories have recently been published by *Black Static* and *Unsung Stories*, although his work has appeared in numerous zines and websites over the years.

Twitter: @steadmanfiction

A.Umbra has been called "the most experimental and avant-garde author since E.L James" by *Blueshit* magazine, while renowned literary critic F. Alse has said "speaking from the shadows of the present, Umbra has shown us the dark corners of the future."

He, she, it, they – I have never seen the face behind the mask – is a shadow that materialises, leaves a puff of lyrical smoke, and disappears into whatever neon hole it came from. Even as his editor, Umbra is extremely difficult to contact due to an intense dislike of any type of personal propaganda. A divorce, caused by an addiction to crying, has only lead to further isolation.

I am writing this with trembling hands. The last time I communicated on Umbra's behalf he threatened to sedate me and melt one of his masks to my face. I knew it wasn't an empty threat when I woke-up with a picture of me decomposing in a jar of clear liquid on the floor beside me – and no memory of what had happened over the last few days…

Adam Worths
Editor for A. Umbra
Email: a.umbra94@gmail.com
Website: www.a-umbra.com

Raised in Italy, Switzerland, Ireland and the UK to Kiwi parents, **Jamie Watt** currently lives on a Ryanair flight somewhere between London and Dublin. He has worked in the film, television and music businesses, but not long enough to become irrevocably cynical.

Jamie studied English at University College Dublin, then worked on a Hollywood film and helped establish a TV channel. He now occasionally works for Ronnie Scott's Jazz Club and is currently writing a Sci-Fi screenplay.

Jamie has a small collection of rare books, an MBA and several dirty secrets. He refuses to submit to the robot overlords.

Email: jamwatt@gmail.com

18219345R00074

Printed in Great Britain
by Amazon